"Ralph stated i̶ **he wished for yo̶̶** **provide your son with a father. Are you in contact with your child's father, and do you intend to marry him in order to claim your inheritance?"**

Cortez did not know why he had asked her when he really wasn't interested in Elin's private life. But he stared at her because he couldn't help himself and waited tensely for her answer. He realized he was bracing himself for her to reply, but when she did he was unprepared for the shock wave that ripped through him.

"You are my son's father," she said in her soft voice that had haunted him for the past year.

The Saunderson Legacy

Jarek and Elin Saunderson had nothing
until they were adopted into the high society
of the Saunderson family.

But following the death of the parents they
adored, they soon discover a maze of secrets that
threaten to destroy their legacy—and lead them
each to uncover unforeseen passions...

Find out more in...

The Secret He Must Claim

A shocking revelation in her adoptive father's will
forces Elin into a marriage of convenience with
the father of her secret baby!

The Throne He Must Take

Playboy Jarek needs help to uncover the secrets
of the past, if he can only resist the temptation
in front of him...Dr. Holly Maitland!

Chantelle Shaw

THE SECRET HE MUST CLAIM

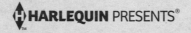

Recycling programs
for this product may
not exist in your area.

ISBN-13: 978-0-373-06090-0

The Secret He Must Claim

First North American Publication 2017

Copyright © 2017 by Chantelle Shaw

Printed in U.S.A.

Chantelle Shaw lives on the Kent coast and thinks up her stories while walking on the beach. She has been married for over thirty years and has six children. Her love affair with reading and writing Harlequin stories began as a teenager, and her first book was published in 2006. She likes strong-willed, slightly unusual characters. Chantelle also loves gardening, walking and wine!

Books by Chantelle Shaw

Harlequin Presents

Acquired by Her Greek Boss
To Wear His Ring Again
A Night in the Prince's Bed
Captive in His Castle
The Ultimate Risk
Ruthless Russian, Lost Innocence

Wedlocked!

Trapped by Vialli's Vows

Bought by the Brazilian

Mistress of His Revenge
Master of Her Innocence

The Howard Sisters

Sheikh's Forbidden Conquest
A Bride Worth Millions

The Chatsfield

Billionaire's Secret

The Bond of Brothers

His Unexpected Legacy
Secrets of a Powerful Man

Visit the Author Profile page at Harlequin.com for more titles.

For Arpita who loves reading romance books as much as I enjoy writing them. Thank you for being such a dedicated fan. With love, Chantelle

CHAPTER ONE

THE ROOM WAS SPINNING. Bright lights flashed in front of her eyes, forming colourful patterns as if she were looking through the lens of a kaleidoscope. Elin blinked and found she was staring up at the chandelier in the drawing room. She had never noticed before how the crystal prisms sparkled like diamonds.

'Can I get you another drink?' A voice sounded over the pounding beat of rock music. She felt disorientated and strangely disembodied, as if she were floating and looking down at herself. She tried to focus on the guy who had spoken to her, and vaguely recognised he was one of Virginia's friends who had been at the nightclub earlier in the evening. Elin didn't know half the people who had come back to her family's London residence in Kensington to continue her birthday celebrations.

'You can't be on your own tonight,' Virginia had insisted when the nightclub where they'd planned to spend the evening had closed early. 'You'll only feel miserable, remembering your mother. I'll put the word around that the party is carrying on back at your place.'

Elin hadn't argued because Virginia was right; she couldn't bear to be alone with the memories of her adoptive mother's shocking death six months ago. She'd told Ralph she was spending her birthday with friends in Scotland, but freezing fog had caused travel disruption at Gatwick and her flight had been cancelled. The person she most wanted to spend her birthday with was her brother, but Jarek was in Japan on business for Saunderson's Bank. His trip was unavoidable he'd said, but Elin had a feeling that Jarek was avoiding her because he blamed himself for Mama's death.

'Elin?'

She jerked her mind back to the guy—Tom, she thought he'd said was his name. He was standing too close and looking at her in a way that made her wish she hadn't worn the daringly low-cut dress Virginia had persuaded her to buy. The dress was little more than a wisp of scarlet silk and chiffon and the shoestring shoulder straps meant she couldn't wear a bra.

Tom plucked her empty glass out of her hand. 'Do you want the same again?'

'I'd better not. I think I've had too much to drink.' This strange feeling must be because she was drunk. It was odd because usually alcohol made her sleepy but she felt wildly energetic and euphoric. The exhausting grief of the past months seemed distant, as if she were detached from her emotions. Maybe the answer was to drink herself into oblivion, the way her brother had done too often lately, Elin thought bleakly. For a split second, misery ripped through her. But she couldn't cope with it tonight. She was desperate to forget for a few hours the image of her mother collapsed on the floor and lying so still. Too still.

'What was in the last cocktail you made me?' she asked Tom. 'It tasted different from a usual Manhattan.'

He gave her an odd look. 'I might have added a dash too much Angostura bitters.' He slid his arm around her waist and Elin repressed a shudder when she felt his hot breath on her cheek. He was good-looking and she guessed a lot of women would find him attractive, but there was something about him that repelled her and she stiffened when he murmured, 'Let's go somewhere where we can be alone, baby.'

'Actually, I would like another drink,' she said quickly. 'I'm really thirsty.' It wasn't a lie. She had a raging thirst, and for some reason her heart was beating unnaturally fast. She watched Tom push his way across the crowded room to the sideboard which was being used as a drinks bar and hurried away before he returned.

In the lounge, someone had rolled up the Wilton rug so that people could dance. The music was even louder in here and the heavy bass throbbed through Elin's body. Someone grabbed her hand and started dancing with her. The pounding beat was irresistible and she shook back her long hair and danced like she'd never danced before, wild and abandoned. Laughter bubbled up inside her. It was a long time since she'd laughed and it felt good.

Many times in the past months she'd tagged along to nightclubs with her brother so she could try to stop him drinking too much. She'd learned that the best way to distract the paparazzi's attention away from Jarek was to grab the limelight herself, and so she'd thrown herself into partying and made sure it was her the press photographed falling out of a club in the early hours rather than her brother.

The tabloids had dubbed her an It Girl and said she was a spoiled socialite. She had been accused by some of the media of bringing shame to Lord Saunderson and to the memory of his wife.

What a way to repay the philanthropic couple who adopted Elin from an orphanage in war-torn Bosnia when she was four years old and gave her and her older brother a privileged upbringing!

That was what one journalist had written. Elin didn't care what the tabloids said about her as long as Jarek's name stayed out of the headlines and he did not earn even more of Ralph's disapproval.

But tonight she wasn't pretending to be having fun. Tonight she felt super-confident and carefree and if it was because she'd had too much alcohol, so what? It was her twenty-fifth birthday and she could do what she liked on her birthday. And so she carried on dancing and laughing because she was scared that if she stopped she would plunge back into that dark place of heartache and grief that had consumed her for six long months.

She had no shortage of dance partners. Men crowded around her and she flirted with them because for this one night she was a siren wearing a sexy red dress. At midnight Virginia brought out a cake covered with candles. 'Don't forget to make a wish,' she reminded Elin.

A birthday wish was supposed to come true if you blew out all your candles with one breath. But a million wishes could not bring Mama back. Elin looked around at the party guests. Some were friends she'd known since her childhood after her adoptive parents had brought her to England. Others she'd never met before, but she guessed they belonged to Virginia's wide circle of friends. Everyone was waiting for her to blow out her candles but she didn't know what to wish for.

And then she saw him.

He was standing apart from the crowd. A lone wolf. The thought came into Elin's mind and was immediately followed by the certainty that he was a dangerous predator. She stared across the room at him…and time simply stopped. The music and voices disappeared and there was nothing but him. The most beautiful man she had ever seen.

Taller than everyone else in the room and darkly handsome, there was something Byronic and brooding about him that made her think of Heathcliff from Emily Brontë's classic novel *Wuthering Heights*. On one level her brain registered surprise that she hadn't noticed him all evening until now, but her rational thought process was overtaken by a more primitive reaction to his raw maleness.

He was dressed in black jeans and a fine-knit black sweater that clung to his broad chest. Over it he wore a brown leather jacket which was scuffed in several places and furthered the impression that he lived life on his terms and didn't give a damn what others thought of him. His black hair was thick and tousled, as if he had a habit of raking his fingers through it, and the black stubble on his jaw and above his top lip added to his smouldering sex appeal.

Something visceral knotted in the pit of Elin's stomach. So this was what desire felt like. This fire in her blood. Her breasts felt heavy and there was a dragging ache between her legs. She *wasn't* a freak, as she'd assumed when her friends had talked about their love lives and she'd had nothing to say.

'Maybe you're gay, but you can't face up to the truth about your sexuality,' Virginia had suggested when Elin had admitted that she was still a virgin.

'The truth is I'm not interested in having sex with anyone. I've dated a few guys but I've never wanted to take things further.' Elin suspected that a psychologist might blame the traumatic first four years of her life spent at an orphanage in the middle of a war zone for her trust issues. Or maybe she *was* frigid, as one ex-boyfriend had told her when he'd failed to persuade her to sleep with him.

Her friend had refused to write her off. 'I reckon you just haven't met the right man yet. One day you'll meet a guy who will flick your switch.'

Was this what Virginia had meant? As Elin stared at this modern-day Heathcliff she felt light and heat and energy explode inside her and suddenly she knew what to wish for when she blew out the candles on her cake.

Someone turned up the volume on the stereo and music pounded in the room, echoing the pounding of Elin's blood in her veins as the crowd around her dispersed and she discovered the man was watching her. He was leaning against the mantelpiece, one foot casually crossed over his other ankle. He gave the appearance of being relaxed but his stillness reminded Elin of a jungle cat preparing to pounce. He did not move his gaze from her when she walked towards him, and it was as if he had taken control of her mind and she could not turn away from him even if she'd wanted to.

His eyes were the colour of sable flecked with gold, she discovered when she halted in front of him. Set beneath heavy black brows that drew together in a faint frown when she smiled at him.

'You're supposed to wish me a happy birthday.' She did not recognise the teasing, flirtatious voice as hers, but then she didn't recognise anything about herself tonight, especially the heat that blazed inside her and made her yearn for something she could not even explain.

Something flickered in his dark eyes but his stern mouth did not soften. 'Happy birthday, Blondie.'

'That's not my name.' She hated the nickname the tabloids had given her, with its implication that because she was pretty and blonde she must also be a brainless bimbo. 'My name is Elin.'

'I know.'

She tilted her head and studied him. The dimmed lighting in the room cast shadows over the hard angles and planes of his face and emphasised his austere beauty, making Elin long to explore the chiselled perfection of his jaw with her fingertips. As for his mouth… Her heart thudded as she imagined his sensual mouth covering hers. The knot in her belly tightened and every nerve-ending in her body felt fiercely alive.

'How do you know my name?' She was certain they'd never met before. Dear God, she would have remembered him.

She wondered if she'd imagined that he hesitated infinitesimally before he shrugged his wide shoulders. 'I'm here at your birthday party and of course I know your name. There can't be many people who haven't heard of Elin Saunderson. Photographs of you falling out of nightclubs are a regular feature in the British popular press.'

Inexplicably she felt hurt by his cynicism, and she was tempted to explain that she'd deliberately courted scandal to turn the media's attention away from her brother. But it would mean betraying Jarek and she would never do that, especially to a stranger. Even if he was the most gorgeous man she'd ever set eyes on. Her gaze locked with his and she saw his gold-flecked eyes blaze with a heat that burned her.

Every one of her heightened senses quivered with the realisation that he desired her. He might not want to want her, but he had no more control over the electricity that crackled between them than she did. He clearly believed she was the goodtime girl portrayed by the press so why shouldn't she live up to her reputation for one night? Elin asked herself.

Some part of her recognised that this wild, reckless feeling wasn't *her*. She shouldn't want a complete stranger to cover her mouth with his and kiss her with the savage passion that she sensed he was capable of. She shouldn't want him, but she did.

'It would be good manners to introduce yourself.'

His mouth quirked then, not exactly a smile but it was enough to send scalding heat flooding through her. 'There's nothing good about me,' he warned her in his deep, dark voice with a faint undercurrent of a Mediterranean accent. Once again he hesitated before he drawled, 'My name is Cortez.'

'You're Spanish?' His dark olive complexion and that raven-black hair indicated that he spent a lot of time in the hot sun. His name—Cor-*tez*... She silently repeated it the way he had pronounced it, emphasising the second syllable. It reminded her of a history book she'd read about the Spanish conquistadors who had invaded the Aztec and Inca civilisations in the sixteenth century. The conquistadors were reputed to have been utterly ruthless and she would be happy to bet that he was a descendent of those infamous adventurers.

'Half-Spanish,' he said after another pause, as if he had been about to say something else but had changed his mind.

She deliberately trailed her eyes over his chest and continued lower, down to his flat abdomen and lean hips, hugged by his black jeans. 'Which half?' she asked innocently.

He looked startled for a few seconds and then laughed. The sound was warm and golden, like liquid honey, Elin thought. '*You* are wicked,' he told her. The bright flecks in his eyes gleamed and something almost feral flickered across his hard features. 'And very, very beautiful.'

He stretched out his hand and wound a lock of her pale gold hair around his fingers. Elin could feel the frantic thud of her heart, and her breath caught in her throat. He must have heard the faint sound, and although he did not appear to move she sensed a sudden tension in him, as if he truly was a predator stalking its prey. He exuded danger and she should run for the hills, but the reckless feeling that had swept over her tonight made her ignore the voice of caution in her head.

The heavy bass music pounding in the room stirred her blood with its sensual rhythm. 'Will you dance with me? You can't refuse,' she said when his eyes narrowed, 'because it's my birthday and I can have whatever I want on my birthday.'

He did not laugh now and the liquid honey in his voice was replaced by a harsh tone that sounded like rusty metal dragged across gravel. 'What *do* you want, Elin?'

'You,' she heard herself say in a husky voice she did not recognise as her own. Once again she felt a peculiar sensation that she was floating outside her body and none of this was real. Perhaps it wasn't, perhaps it was a dream, but it was a much better dream than her usual nightmare about her mother's death.

Cortez swore softly. The gold flecks in his eyes glittered and he seemed to be waging an internal battle with himself before he shrugged. 'So be it then,' he muttered as he moved towards her. He put his hands on her waist and pulled her against him so that they were hip to hip.

The effect on Elin was electrifying. The brush of his thighs against hers as they moved with the beat of the music turned the heat inside her into an inferno. Cortez danced with a fluid grace that was entirely sensual, and she gasped when he slid one hand down to the small of her back and exerted pressure to bring her pelvis into closer contact with his.

Her senses went into meltdown as he clamped her against his whipcord body. He smelled divine, a mixture of spicy cologne and the dry heat of his body that had its own unique scent. She wanted to press her face into his neck and breathe in the essence of him, lick his olive skin and taste him. Her hands were lying flat on his chest and she felt his heartbeat accelerate beneath her fingertips. Startled, she tilted her head to look at his face, and saw a stark hunger in his eyes that made her tremble.

She'd never felt like this before and she'd certainly never behaved so impetuously. She felt crazily out of control. For the first time in six months she felt alive instead of numb. Life, she'd learned, could be taken away in an instant, in the release of a trigger and a bullet fired from a gun.

She wanted to grab hold of life with both hands, and more than anything she wanted to be even closer to this dangerously beautiful man who made her feel like no other man ever had. And so she slid her hands up to his shoulders and stretched herself up against him, pressing her breasts with their pebble-hard nipples into his chest. She heard him mutter something in Spanish as he sank his hand into her hair and lowered his face towards hers. His mouth was tantalisingly close and with a low moan she closed the tiny gap between them and pressed her lips to his.

The world exploded in a firestorm of heat and

colour. Cortez hesitated for a fraction of a second but then a shudder went through him and he took control of the kiss and plundered her mouth like a conquistador claiming the spoils of his conquest. It was hotter and wilder than anything Elin had ever experienced before. She felt consumed by his kiss, by him as he moved his hand to cup her jaw and angled her mouth to his satisfaction before he pushed his tongue between her lips and tasted her.

The kiss went on and on, becoming deeper and ever more erotic, a ravishment of her senses, and Elin hoped it would never end. When Cortez eventually tore his mouth from hers to allow them to snatch air into their starved lungs, he stared at her as if he was trying to figure her out.

'This is madness,' he grated. 'I should tell you…' He broke off when one of the other guests who was dancing wildly stumbled into them. *'Dios!'* Cortez tightened his arms around Elin and his protective gesture made her melt even more. 'Is there somewhere we can go to talk?'

Over Cortez's shoulder, Elin saw Tom, the guy who had been plying her with drinks earlier, walk into the room. Keen to avoid him, she led Cortez through a different door to the narrow hallway and staircase at the back of the house, which had once been used by servants. Even here there were people sitting on the stairs playing a raucous drinking game, and so she continued up to the second floor and along the corridor to her bedroom.

'We won't be disturbed in here,' she told him as she ushered him inside and closed the door. After the loud music downstairs the room was quiet, with just the distant thud of heavy bass audible through the floorboards. On some level Elin knew she must be crazy to have invited a stranger into her bedroom. Except that he wasn't a complete stranger, she reassured herself. She knew his name and she assumed Virginia knew him. Why else would he have come to the party unless her friend had invited him?

Even so, a tiny, sane part of her realised she was acting a little bit crazy tonight. She couldn't explain the buzz of exhilaration that felt as if she were riding on a big dipper at a theme park, but she didn't want the feeling to end. She stared at Cortez and thought how unbelievably gorgeous he was. No wonder Virginia had kept quiet about him. But he had kissed *her*.

In the mirror she could see her mouth was swollen from when he had crushed her lips beneath his. She hardly recognised herself in a sexy scarlet dress, with her hair dishevelled and her mouth reddened… and inviting. She looked back at Cortez and watched his eyes narrow as she moistened her lips with the tip of her tongue.

'You said you wanted to tell me something. Are you married?'

'*What?*' He looked startled. 'No, of course not. I would not have kissed you if I were married.'

'Why *did* you kiss me?'

'Why the hell do you think?' he said roughly.

'I'm not sure. Perhaps you should kiss me again and I might work out the reason.' There it was again, that teasing, flirty voice that she didn't recognise as her own. But the truth was she wanted him to kiss her, and she wanted more. She wanted… Her eyes flicked to the huge double bed that she'd only ever slept in alone. She heard Cortez mutter something incomprehensible as he followed her gaze.

'You are an irresistible temptation.' He made it sound like an accusation as he closed the gap between them in a couple of strides. Her bedroom seemed to shrink and she could not tear her gaze from him. The golden gleam in his eyes promised he would make her birthday wish come true.

'Are you going to resist me?' she murmured when he stood in front of her and cupped her cheek in his big hand. The skin on his palm felt rough and she wondered briefly what he did for a living.

'Not a chance,' he growled as he pulled her against him, into his heat and strength and intoxicating maleness, and claimed her mouth in a kiss that plundered her soul.

'Do you want this?' he demanded, lifting his head and staring into her eyes as if he was trying to read her thoughts.

'Do you have to ask?' replied the voice she didn't recognise that belonged to the bold creature who had taken over her body. It was *that* woman who wound her arms around his neck and pulled his mouth down to hers—a scarlet-clad temptress who murmured words of encouragement when he lifted her up and placed her on the bed before he stretched out on top of her.

His weight pinned her to the mattress and his muscular body felt alien and hard against her softness. He kissed her mouth, demanding a response she gave willingly. She wanted everything he could give her, and her urgency increased when he trailed his lips down her throat.

Their clothes were a frustrating barrier and she pushed his jacket over his shoulders while he tugged the straps of her dress down her arms. There was the sound of material ripping and then the feel of cool air on her bare breasts.

She moaned when he bent his dark head to her breast and took her nipple into his mouth. The sensation of him sucking her was exquisite, and flames shot down from her breasts to the molten place between her legs as he transferred his mouth to her other nipple and tugged on the taut crest.

'Please...' she choked. Instinct took over and she lifted her hips towards him as he thrust a hand beneath her skirt and skimmed his palm over the sensitive skin of her inner thigh. He dragged her panties down her legs, and then his fingers were there where she was desperate for him to touch her, probing her slick heat before he slid one digit, two, into her and moved them expertly so that within moments she was trembling on the brink.

'I want…' she gasped. She had never felt desire like this before, so fierce and urgent, making her shake with need.

'I know.' His voice was like rough velvet. He kissed her mouth again and in between hungry kisses he pulled his sweater over his head. His skin felt like satin overlaid with wiry chest hairs that scraped her palms as she moved her hands down to the zip of his jeans.

Everything was colour and heat and fierce, frantic need that built in intensity as he swirled his fingers inside her. Somehow Cortez was naked and the sight of his erection made Elin draw a swift breath. He was awesome—so beautiful, so *big*. But her faint doubt was obliterated when he twisted his fingers inside her and she shattered, her orgasm so overwhelming that she gave a keening cry.

'I don't have a condom.' His harsh voice broke through the haze of sexual excitement fogging her brain and she heard him swear as he lifted himself off her. *She didn't want him to stop.* Frantically she clutched his shoulders and remembered the packet of condoms which had been given out for free when she had been a fresher at university. She had shoved them into the bedside drawer, wondering if she would ever need them.

'In the top drawer,' she muttered.

It took him mere moments to locate the packet and don a protective sheath before he positioned himself over her and nudged her legs apart with his thigh.

And then he entered her with a hard thrust that made her gasp. The slight discomfort was over almost immediately. She felt him hesitate, but the sensation of being stretched by him and filled by his steel-hard length was so incredible that she arched her hips and urged him to possess her utterly.

The intense pleasure of her first orgasm made her greedy for more and she dug her fingers into his shoulders, anchoring herself to his powerful body as he drove into her again and again, taking her higher and making her sob with need, until finally the world exploded and she heard him groan as together they fell over the edge of the abyss.

Elin stirred and the light hurt her eyes before she'd even opened them. Cautiously, she lifted her lashes and winced as a shaft of bright sunshine fell across her face. Her head felt strangely woolly and it took several minutes to register that she was in her bedroom at the house in Kensington. She pushed back the sheet and discovered she'd fallen into bed wearing her dress. The top half was pushed down around her waist, leaving her breasts bare, and when she moved her hand lower she discovered that her knickers were missing.

Dear God! Vague memories swirled in her mind. There had been a party, loud music, candles on a cake. She remembered dancing with various men— with one man in particular. A savagely handsome man with jet-black hair and gold-flecked eyes who had said his name was Cortez.

She jerked upright and the room spun. Her stomach churned but her symptoms didn't feel like a hangover. Patches of her memory of the previous night were blank but others were shudderingly vivid. She remembered that she'd danced with Cortez and they had kissed. Embarrassed heat flooded her cheeks when she recalled that *she* had initiated the kiss before she'd invited him up to her room.

What else had she done?

She spied her knickers on the floor and the answer hit her in a tidal wave of shame. She'd had sex for the first time in her life with a man she'd never met before, and the fact that she had woken alone at—the clock showed it was midday—suggested that Cortez had long since gone.

'Elin, are you in there?' Virginia's voice sounded from outside the door.

'Just a minute.' She grabbed her robe and pulled it on over her crumpled dress, desperate to hide the evidence of her night of shame. Virginia was her best friend but Elin did not want to tell anyone what she'd done, how she'd behaved like a slut. She wanted to crawl away and hide in a hole, but she forced herself to smile when she opened her bedroom door.

'Are you alone?' Virginia sounded surprised. 'I saw you disappear from the party with a gorgeous guy and thought maybe you'd spent the night with him. Who was he?'

'He said his name was Cortez.' Elin swallowed. 'I didn't get round to asking his surname. But I thought he was a friend of yours. Didn't you invite him to the party?'

'I'd never seen him before he turned up here last night.' Virginia frowned. 'It's a bit odd. I haven't spoken to anyone who was at the party who knows him.'

Virginia dismissed the mystery of Cortez's identity with an airy shrug that Elin envied. 'You missed all the drama last night. A guy called Tom Wilson was arrested on suspicion of spiking my friend Lisa's drink. Apparently she felt strange after drinking a cocktail Tom had made her but she assumed she was drunk. A while later he tried to get Lisa to leave the party with him, but someone else warned her that they'd seen Tom slip something into her drink. The police were called, and when they tested the dregs of drink in the bottom of Lisa's glass they found evidence of a substance which is a well-known date-rape drug.'

Something clicked in Elin's mind and she sank down onto the bed. 'Do you know what the effects of taking the drug are?'

'Lisa said she felt dizzy and out of control and she described feeling detached from reality. Oh, my God,' Virginia said in a horrified voice as she noticed Elin's white face. 'Do you think your drink was spiked too?'

'Tom made me a cocktail and I felt strange after drinking it. But, like Lisa, I thought I was drunk.'

'You had better inform the police that it's possible you were another of Tom's victims. Some so-called date-rape drugs can cause blackouts and amnesia and if you unwittingly took the drug it would explain why you've been asleep for half the day.'

If her drink had been spiked it would explain her bizarre, out-of-character behaviour last night. But it was a cold comfort, Elin thought grimly. Cortez would have been unaware that she'd been drugged. However, he'd mentioned her reputation as an It Girl—how she detested the label—and he had clearly believed she made a habit of sleeping with men she'd just met. The fact that he had disappeared after they'd had sex, without waking her, made her feel like a tramp.

As soon as Virginia had gone, Elin stripped off the scarlet dress that had become her badge of shame and shoved it into the bin. She felt soiled, but when she took a shower no amount of hot water and soap could scrub away her self-loathing or the marks on her body left by Cortez. Padding from the en suite bathroom back into her bedroom, she stood in front of the mirror and allowed the towel she'd wrapped around her to fall.

The evidence of her guilt was branded on her body. There were red patches on her breasts where Cortez's rough jaw had scraped her delicate skin, and although there were no visible signs of the ache between her legs, the dull throb was an uncomfortable reminder that she had lost her virginity having casual sex with a stranger.

Thank God he had used a condom. Elin held her hands to her hot cheeks and wished she *did* have amnesia. But memories of her wanton behaviour were painfully clear in her mind. Cortez hadn't forced her or coerced her to have sex with him, and even discovering that her drink might have been spiked by another of the party guests did not make her feel any better about herself. She'd behaved like a whore, and her only consolation was that she was unlikely to meet the Spanish conquistador who had taken her self-respect along with her virginity ever again.

CHAPTER TWO

One year later

AN ICY BLAST of air swept into the church and the ancient oak door creaked on its hinges, heralding the arrival of a latecomer to Ralph Saunderson's funeral. Sitting in a front pew beside her brother, Elin felt the cold draught curl around her ankles and wished she'd worn her boots. But her black patent four-inch stilettos looked better with her nineteen-fifties style coat and matching black pillbox hat with a net veil that the milliner had said made her look like Grace Kelly, and Elin had learned when she was four years old that looks were everything.

A faint frown creased between her perfectly arched brows as she listened to footsteps ring out on the stone floor of the nave. When she and Jarek had followed their adoptive father's coffin into the church she'd noted that every pew was filled. It seemed as though the entire population of Little Bardley had turned out to bid farewell to the squire of the pretty Sussex village on the South Downs. Elin had made a mental note of the many familiar faces in the congregation so that she could thank each person who had attended the funeral.

Who had arrived halfway through the service? She felt a prickling sensation between her shoulder blades and although she tried to concentrate on the minister while he gave the eulogy, she could not dismiss an inexplicable sense of unease. When the congregation stood to sing a hymn, she glanced over her shoulder and her heart collided with her ribs when she thought she recognised the man standing at the back of the church.

Cortez!

It couldn't be him. Elin drew a shaky breath. Her brain must be playing a cruel trick on her. It was over a year since her fateful birthday party when she'd had sex with a stranger who she'd known only as Cortez. There was no reason in the world why he would have turned up at her father's funeral.

She jerked her head round to the front and stared down at the hymn book that shook uncontrollably between her fingers. Her brother swore softly as he slid his hand beneath her arm.

'You're not going to faint, are you?' Jarek muttered. 'The press pack who are slavering outside the church would love to snap you being carried unconscious from a venue for the second time this week. Of course there would be speculation in the tabloids that you were drunk or high at your dear papa's funeral.'

'You know I'm neither,' Elin said in a low voice,

while the congregation sang the second verse of the hymn. 'I explained that I fainted at Virginia's hen party two nights ago because it was so hot and stuffy in the nightclub.'

'A more likely explanation is that you are still not fully recovered from Harry's traumatic birth. I know he is three months old, but you lost God knows how many pints of blood when you haemorrhaged after giving birth,' her brother said grimly. 'I told you before you went to London that I didn't think you were fit enough to return to your frenetic social life.'

Elin was stung by the faint censure in his words. The only reason she had become a familiar face on the London club scene a year ago had been so that she could try and keep Jarek out of trouble and out of the tabloids' headlines. At least she no longer had to worry that Ralph would lose patience with her brother. Their adoptive father had died a week ago, a month after being diagnosed with a brain tumour. Jarek was destined to take over as head of Saunderson's Bank and even though many of the bank's board members were concerned by his reputation as a risk-taker, no one could prevent Ralph Saunderson's heir from becoming chairman.

Elin bowed her head while the minister intoned a prayer, but her mind was on the man she'd seen in the church. She'd only caught a glimpse of him, and of course he couldn't be Cortez, she reassured herself. Although he had known her name and London address, he had never tried to contact her in the past year and, as she did not know his surname, she'd been unable to find him to tell him about Harry.

She thought of her baby son, who had been asleep when she'd left him with his nanny in the nursery at Cuckmere Hall. Harry was innocently unaware that he had been conceived as a result of a few moments of lust between two strangers. But when he was older he was bound to be curious about his father, and Elin planned to make up a story that Harry's father was dead. It would be better to tell her son a white lie than for him to learn that his father had abandoned him before his birth, she reasoned.

She and her brother had been abandoned by their own parents when she was a baby. Jarek had been six and he had a few vague memories of their mother and father. But Elin's earliest memories were of looking through the bars of a cot. Jarek had told her that at the orphanage the younger children had been left in their cots, often for days. She hadn't learned to walk until she was over two years old, and only then because her brother had sneaked into her dormitory and held her hand while she took her first steps.

Her own son had been conceived as a result of her night of shame with a stranger, but she was determined to love Harry twice as much to make up for the fact that he would never know his father.

The ceremony finished and she walked with Jarek behind Ralph's coffin as it was carried out of the chapel. She looked closely at the people in the congregation but did not see anyone who resembled Cortez.

Her imagination must have played a trick on her, she told herself, yet her sense of unease remained.

The procession of mourners filed into the grave-yard and gathered around a freshly dug grave next to Lorna Saunderson's headstone. Tears welled in Elin's eyes. It was eighteen months since Mama had died and she still felt a deep sense of loss. Willing herself not to cry in public, she stared across the graveyard, and her heart lurched when she glimpsed a tall figure half-hidden behind the thick trunk of an old yew tree. She could not see the man's features clearly from a distance, but something about his proud bearing and the breadth of his shoulders were familiar.

She blinked away her tears and refocused but the figure had disappeared. A flock of crows flew out of the tree, cawing loudly as if something had disturbed them. Had she imagined that she'd seen someone? Elin forced herself to concentrate on the minister reciting a final prayer, and when he finished she stepped forwards and dropped a white rose into her father's grave.

'You look like you've seen a ghost,' her brother told her later when they arrived back at Cuckmere Hall. 'The old man is more likely to come back to haunt me than you. He did at least feel some affec-tion for you,' he added drily. 'Ralph wanted to adopt a pretty little daughter but he was less keen to take on a ten-year-old boy with issues.' Jarek strode into the house and took a glass of sherry from the butler, who was waiting in the entrance hall to greet them.

'Ralph cared for both of us,' Elin murmured, telling herself it was true. Admittedly she had not felt the close bond with her adoptive father that she'd had with Lorna Saunderson, but she'd been fond of the man who had been the only father she'd ever known. However, Jarek had struggled to settle into his new life in England and to accept Ralph's authority.

'We were his social experiment. Take a couple of kids from the lowest tier of society and see if he could mould them to fit in with the gentility.' Jarek gave a sardonic smile. 'It's fair to say that Ralph had more success with you than with me.'

'That's not true. I'm sure he thought highly of you, and he respected your financial flair, which is why he appointed you in a senior position at Saunderson's Bank.'

Elin took off her hat and coat and smoothed a crease from her black pencil dress. She declined the glass of sherry the butler offered her. 'Baines, I noticed there is a car parked on the driveway. I presume that my father's solicitor is here?' She had hoped to run up to the nursery and spend five minutes with Harry, but she would have to wait until after the formal reading of Ralph's will.

'Mr Carstairs and his associate arrived ten minutes ago and I showed the gentlemen into the library.'

'Business must be doing well for old Carstairs to drive an Aston Martin,' Jarek commented. 'I suppose he's brought a trainee from the law firm with him, but there wasn't much point. Ralph had no other family apart from us and his will must be straight-forward. At least the reading of the will shouldn't take long,' he said, glancing at his watch. 'I'm racing later this afternoon.'

'I wish you wouldn't race that damned motorbike,' Elin muttered as she followed her brother across the hallway. 'It's such a risky sport.'

'Everything carries an element of risk.' A nerve jumped in Jarek's jaw. 'No one could have predicted that a trip to a jewellers would cost Mama her life.'

Elin was saved from answering as she entered the library and Peter Carstairs immediately got up from an armchair. 'Elin, Jarek, I am sure this is a difficult day for you and I will endeavour not to take up too much of your time.'

'Thank you.' Elin wondered why the normally affable solicitor seemed tense. 'Would you like a drink?'

'No, thank you. I think we should proceed.' Mr Carstairs moved to the chair behind the desk and Elin followed her brother over to the sofa. She suddenly remembered that Baines had said he had shown two men into the library, but before she could suggest that they wait until the solicitor's clerk returned—presumably he was visiting the cloakroom—Mr Carstairs picked up a document and began to read from it.

He began by announcing several small bequests that Ralph Saunderson had made to members of the household staff. 'Next we come to the Saunderson's estate winery.' The solicitor cleared his throat. 'I leave a fifty per cent share of the vineyards and winery to my adopted daughter Elin Dvorska Saunderson.'

Elin felt a jolt of surprise. She had assumed that Ralph would hand the entire ownership of the estate winery to her. She'd worked as production manager for the past eighteen months and was committed to fulfilling Lorna Saunderson's vision of producing world class English sparkling wine. Jarek had never shown any interest in the vineyards and winery, but perhaps Ralph had hoped his heir would become more involved in developing Saunderson's Wines, she reasoned.

She was vaguely aware of the library door opening and heard a faint click as it closed again, but her attention was on Mr Carstairs and she did not look round to see who had entered the room. The solicitor gave another nervous cough. 'There is a stipulation attached to the bequest, Elin. Mr Saunderson decreed that you must marry within one year and provide your son with a father before you can claim your inheritance. If you choose not to fulfil the obligation, your share of Saunderson's Wines will revert to your adoptive father's main heir.'

Shock rendered Elin speechless. She knew her adoptive father had disapproved of her being a single mother but once Harry had been born he'd seemed delighted with the baby. 'I can't believe Ralph would really have expected me to meet the terms of his will,' she said at last in a shaky voice. 'Or that a judge would uphold such an outrageous stipulation if I contested the will.'

'Mr Saunderson was completely within his rights to distribute his assets in any manner he saw fit,' the solicitor murmured. 'I have to advise you that there are no grounds on which you could contest your father's wishes.'

Her brother reached over and squeezed Elin's hand. 'You know Ralph liked to play his little games,' he said sardonically. 'This is just his way of trying to maintain control from beyond the grave. Don't worry, Ellie. Your share of the wine business will come to me if you haven't married in a year and I'll sign the whole of Saunderson's Wines over to you. I have no desire to toil in the vineyards.' Jarek glanced at the solicitor. 'Do you mind getting on with it? I have other things to do today.'

Mr Carstairs cleared his throat again. 'There are only two further items.' He continued to read the will. 'I leave two properties, Rose Cottage and Ivy Cottage, to my adopted children, Jarek and Elin, to live in or dispose of according to their wishes.'

Why had Ralph made the odd bequest? Elin's feeling of unease grew. It did not make sense. Her brother was Ralph's heir and would inherit the entire Cuckmere estate, which included Cuckmere Hall, two thousand acres of Sussex farmland, woodland and vineyards, plus thirty-five cottages and the pub in Little Bardley. She knotted her fingers together in her lap while Mr Carstairs continued.

'Finally, I give everything I own at my death, excluding the aforementioned bequests, all monies and properties and also the position of chairman of Saunderson's Bank, of which it is my right to appoint my successor, to my only natural son, Cortez Ramos.'

Silence. Lasting for what felt like a lifetime. Elin pressed her hand to her chest to try and ease the violent thud of her heart as the solicitor's words reverberated around her head.

Cortez.

It couldn't be the Cortez she'd had sex with a year ago. It must be a ghastly coincidence, she frantically told herself. But her sense of dread intensified when she remembered the dark figure she'd caught sight of in the graveyard. What did Ralph's astonishing will mean for her and Jarek? For her son? Her heart felt as if it would jump out of her chest. Fear, she realised. The certainty of the future that she had taken for granted had just been blown apart.

She was aware that her brother had stiffened but as always he kept tight control over his emotions. 'Is this some kind of joke, Carstairs?' Jarek drawled. 'You know full well that Ralph and Lorna Saunderson were unable to have children and so they adopted my sister and I. Ralph did not have a natural son and this Cortez Ramos, whoever he is, cannot have any legal claim to my adoptive father's estate.'

Before Mr Carstairs could reply, a voice spoke from the back of the room. A deep voice with a husky accent that Elin had heard too often in her dreams in the past year. 'Ralph did not have a *legitimate* natural son, but he had a bastard.' The voice became harsh. 'I am Ralph Saunderson's biological son and heir.'

Elin felt her stomach twist. *This can't be happening*, she thought, prayed. *If I turn my head, he won't be there and this whole nightmare will have been a dream.* She jerked her head round and her heart juddered to a standstill. At her birthday party a year ago she'd thought him the most beautiful man she'd ever seen, but Cortez was even more stunning than her memories of him.

'So it *was* you I saw in the church,' she choked. 'I thought I'd recognised you, but there was no reason why you should be there…or so I believed.' Her voice dropped to a whisper as the shock of seeing him stole her breath from her lungs.

Jarek had leapt up from the sofa. He looked at Cortez and back to Elin. 'Do you know this man?'

She swallowed, desperately trying to block out the images in her mind of Cortez's naked, powerfully muscular body poised above her as she lay sprawled on her bed at the house in Kensington. His dark olive skin a stark contrast to her paleness as he pushed her dress up around her waist and nudged her thighs apart. A bold conquistador laying claim to his prize. At least all that sleek, hard beauty was clothed today, but the formality of his charcoal-grey suit that he wore with a black shirt and tie did not lessen the impact of his raw masculinity.

'We…we met once,' she managed. The gold flecks

in Cortez's dark eyes gleamed with what Elin furiously recognised was amusement. Never had she been more grateful for her reserved English upbringing with its emphasis on controlling her emotions. 'It was an unmemorable event,' she said coolly.

Her brother frowned. 'Did you know of his alleged relationship to Ralph?'

'Of course not.' The faint suspicion in Jarek's eyes felt like a knife in her heart. She owed her life to her brother. If it hadn't been for him, God knew what would have happened to her when Sarajevo had been attacked and a bomb had landed on the orphanage. 'If I'd had any inkling I would have told you.'

Elin bit her lip as her brother strode across the library and flung open the door. 'Jarek—where are you going?' She carefully did not look at Cortez as she hurried past him, but she was conscious of his tall, brooding presence and the evocative spicy scent of his aftershave tugged on her senses.

'You know why Ralph has done this, don't you?' Jarek said bitterly when Elin caught up with him in the entrance hall. 'He blamed me for Mama's death. And he was right. I should have saved her.'

'There was nothing you could have done against an armed raider. It wasn't your fault. Jarek…' Elin's hand fell from her brother's arm as he spun away from her and grabbed his motorbike helmet from the hall table.

'If I hadn't tried to be a hero, Lorna would still be here. I took a gamble when I tackled the gunman, but the gamble failed. I understand why Ralph excluded me from his will but he had no reason to cut you out.' Jarek opened the front door and turned to face her. 'Do you know what I wish?' he said rawly. 'I wish that when we were held hostage in the raid on the jewellers the goddamned gunman had shot me instead of Mama. It's obvious that's what Ralph wished.'

'Oh, please be careful.' Elin wanted to go after her brother when he ran down the front steps and leapt onto his motorbike parked on the drive, but Peter Carstairs came out of the library and spoke to her.

'Mr Ramos was kind enough to give me a lift here and I arranged for a taxi to collect me,' he said as a car turned onto the driveway. 'I'm sorry to have been the harbinger of bad news, my dear. This must all be a great shock.'

The solicitor was the master of the understatement, Elin thought with a flash of macabre humour. 'My father died from a brain tumour. Is it possible that he was not of sound mind when he made Cortez Ramos his heir? Do we even know for sure that Mr Ramos is Ralph's son?'

She tensed when she saw Cortez standing in the doorway of the library and realised he must have overheard her. Too bad, she thought grimly. She was fighting for her and her brother's inheritance and, more importantly, for her son's future.

Harry was Cortez's son.

Oh, God, she couldn't think about the implications now, or how she was going to break the news to the granite-faced stranger she'd had sex with one time that he had fathered a child. She heard Jarek's motorbike roar off down the drive and a knot of fear for his safety tightened in her stomach.

The solicitor shook his head. 'Mr Saunderson was definitely of sound mind when he asked me to draw up a new will for him six months or so after his wife's death. I believe he had suspected for some time that Mr Ramos could be his son and when a DNA test proved it, he invited his son here to Cuckmere Hall. He asked me to draw up the new will on the same day that Mr Ramos visited, on the third of March a year ago.'

'The third of March is my birthday,' Elin said faintly. The realisation that her adoptive father had written his extraordinary will, which effectively left her penniless, on her birthday, felt like a devastating betrayal. There was no possibility of her marrying within a year so that she could claim a fifty per cent share of Saunderson's Wines.

She felt bombarded by one shock after another, and on top of the worry about her future she was terrified that her brother would risk his life riding his motorbike dangerously fast. She felt the same sensation of being unable to breathe that she'd experienced two nights ago in a crowded nightclub. Her legs buckled beneath her, and as if from a long way off she heard Cortez swear.

CHAPTER THREE

ELIN WEIGHED NEXT to nothing, Cortez discovered as he sprang forwards and caught her before she hit the floor. Her fragility was the first thing that had struck him when he'd seen her standing at the front of the church. Was her slender figure the result of dieting to be fashionably thin, or was there a more sinister reason? he wondered as he strode into the library with her in his arms.

Two days ago, pictures of her being carried out of a London nightclub had been plastered over the front pages of the tabloids. There had been speculation that she'd taken cocaine or another recreational drug, popular on the club scene. *Is this proof that Elin has resumed her party lifestyle?* had been one headline.

Cortez had been annoyed with himself for pandering to his curiosity and buying the newspaper to read the full story. The references to Elin's party girl reputation of a year ago, before she had mysteriously dropped off the paparazzi's radar for a few months, had made him shove the paper into the rubbish bin in disgust.

What the hell had possessed him to have sex with her when he'd unwittingly gatecrashed her party? The answer felt like a punch in his gut. The same punch that had made him catch his breath when he'd watched her dancing at her party. *Desire*. Uncontrollable, ferocious desire had shot through him like a lightning bolt.

Unbidden memories pushed into his mind of Elin wearing a low-cut red dress that barely covered her pert breasts. Her pale blonde hair fell in a silken curtain around her shoulders, framing her exquisite face with its elfin features and a wide mouth that was entirely sensual. The moment he'd seen her he'd been unable to take his eyes off her. Even knowing what she was—a spoilt little rich girl who cared about nothing other than where the next party was being held and—if the press stories about her were true—where she could get her next fix—hadn't lessened his hunger for her.

It was a little over twelve months ago when he had come to England after he'd received the result of a DNA test which confirmed he was Ralph Saunderson's son. Ralph had invited him to Cuckmere Hall, and Cortez had gone because he could not deny he was curious to meet his biological father, who had abandoned his mother when she was pregnant. He had already discovered that Ralph was wealthy and the Saundersons were an old aristocratic family.

Driving through the vast Cuckmere estate on his way up to the mansion, Cortez had felt bitter remembering how his mother had worked herself literally into an early grave. Thirty-five years ago, Marisol Ramos had been pregnant and alone, abandoned by her lover and shunned by her family in Spain. She had managed to establish a small vineyard in Andalucía and from almost as soon as Cortez could walk he had helped his mother tend the vines and harvest the grapes. The bodega had produced a fine sherry, but it couldn't compete with the big sherry producers in the sherry triangle in south-west Spain. Life had been hard, and when his mother had died at the age of forty-two Cortez had been convinced that she'd simply felt too exhausted to carry on living.

When he had finally met Ralph Saunderson the only emotion he'd felt was anger that his father had consigned his mother to a life of poverty and hardship. At the time of his visit to Cuckmere Hall the English press had been full of stories about Ralph's adopted son and daughter's jet set lifestyle, in particular Elin's wild partying. But the pictures of her in the newspapers and her photo on Ralph's desk that had caught Cortez's attention had not prepared him for the impact she had on him when he saw her dancing at her birthday party.

He jerked his mind from the past as Elin's eyelashes fluttered open. For a few seconds she stared at him with her dark blue eyes that had reminded him of sapphires when he'd danced with her a year ago. He recalled how she had pressed her body up close to his. As close as she was now, except that then she had been soft and pliant in his arms and she'd parted her lush mouth in an invitation he had been unable to resist.

That should have been a warning, he thought grimly. He never had a problem resisting women. He was always in control and when he took a mistress it was always on his terms, with rules and boundaries established first. Falling into bed with Elin had broken every rule he'd imposed on himself since he'd fallen in love with Alandra in his early twenties and she had shattered his illusions about love and his own judgement.

'What are you doing? Put me down.'

Cortez heard panic in Elin's voice and he felt a stab of irritation when he lowered her onto the sofa and she immediately recoiled from him as if he were infected with a contagious disease. She hadn't behaved like that a year ago, he brooded. She'd been all over him then. He walked across to the desk, where the butler had left a tray of drinks, and tried to dismiss the memory of Elin sprawled on a bed with her red dress rucked up around her waist and her pale thighs spread wide open.

'Here,' he said curtly, returning to hand her a glass of brandy.

She shook her head. 'I never touch spirits and in fact I rarely drink alcohol at all.'

How could she look so damned *innocent* when he had irrefutable proof that she was far from it? He remembered how she had flirted with him at her birthday party and he had been blown away by her sexual allure.

Cortez's anger with himself increased when he found he could not tear his eyes away from Elin. She was even more beautiful than he remembered. The black dress she was wearing was a classic style reminiscent of a previous era when women had looked effortlessly elegant. Her pale blonde hair was swept up into a chignon that emphasised the incredible bone structure of her face, with those high cheekbones and perfectly arched brows above the bluest eyes he'd ever seen. He felt a sudden tightness in his chest and to his fury he was powerless to control the almost painful throb of his sexual arousal.

'If you were not drunk when you had to be carried out of a nightclub the other night, then perhaps the recent lurid tabloid headlines alleging that you have a drug habit are true,' he drawled.

Colour stained her porcelain cheeks. 'The press print a lot of lies about me, but the truth is that I fainted in the nightclub because I've been unwell recently. I felt wobbly just now because it was a huge shock to learn that my father had excluded me and my brother from his will, and named you— his illegitimate son that no one knew existed—as his heir.' Elin's voice was icy but her eyes flashed with fury as she got up from the sofa and faced him.

'Did you go to the house in Kensington and gatecrash my party so you could gloat? Ralph must have told you a year ago that he intended to make you his heir. Wasn't it enough to know you would inherit Cuckmere Hall, the house in London and the chairmanship of Saunderson's Bank, and you decided you would take me too?'

Cortez gave a hard smile, because here at last was proof that she might look like an angel, with her golden beauty and that ridiculous air of innocence that made his gut twist, but she was just another blonde who had satisfied his libido for a few hours, and she was no different to all the other blondes who regarded sex as a bartering tool. No doubt if he had stuck around after they'd slept together, Elin would have issued demands the way all women did.

'As a matter of fact I did not know about the will,' he told her. 'After I met my father for the first time at Cuckmere Hall I had planned to spend the night at a hotel in London, but Ralph suggested I could stay at his house in Kensington and gave me a key. He said that you and your brother were both abroad and the house would be empty. When I walked into your party I had every intention of leaving, but you begged me to dance with you.'

Cortez was fascinated by the tide of scarlet that swept along her high cheekbones. 'I did not take anything that was not offered freely,' he said harshly. 'You invited me into your bedroom and made it clear that you wanted sex.' He shrugged. 'Knowing of your reputation, I don't flatter myself that I was your first or last one-night stand.'

The colour receded from her face. 'You really *are*

a bastard, aren't you? That night I was under the influence of a drug which impaired my judgement and caused me to behave in a way I would never normally have done. As for my reputation—' she gave a short laugh '—you know nothing about me.'

There was a strained note of what he could almost believe was *hurt* in her voice that made Cortez feel uncomfortable. He had no reason to feel guilty, he assured himself. Elin had just admitted that she'd taken drugs at her party and implied that she'd had sex with him because she had been high. But he'd been unaware she'd taken any kind of substance or that her behaviour was out of character. Everything he'd read about her in the press suggested she'd had many previous sex partners.

Memories of that night were crystal-clear in his mind, despite the distance of a year. He remembered that when he had pulled her beneath him and thrust himself into her with a desperation he'd never felt before, she had tensed and caught her breath. *Dios*, she had been so tight and so goddamned hot that he'd almost come instantly. But then she'd wrapped her legs around his hips and matched his pace when he began to move. Passion had blazed between them and he'd dismissed the unlikely notion that she was sexually inexperienced.

Maybe it was an act she put on with other men, Cortez thought darkly. He had proof that he could not have been her first lover.

'I know you have a child.' He wondered why he

felt a simmering rage at the thought of her slender body wrapped around another man. He had been shocked when he'd heard during the reading of Ralph's will that Elin had a son. It was odd the media had not reported that she had a child.

'Ralph stated in his will that he wished for you to marry and provide your son with a father. Are you in contact with your child's father, and do you intend to marry him in order to claim your inheritance?'

He did not know why he had asked her when he really wasn't interested in her private life. But he stared at her because he couldn't help himself and waited tensely for her answer. He realised he was bracing himself for her to reply, but when she did he was unprepared for the shockwave that ripped through him.

'*You* are my son's father,' she said in her soft voice that had haunted him for the past year.

For a split second he wondered if it was possible, but… 'No.' He dismissed the idea. 'You can't pin the blame on me. Although I can see why it would be convenient if I was the father of your child,' he said sardonically. 'I would feel duty-bound to marry you, and you need a husband in order to meet the terms of Ralph's will. Marriage to me would give you not only a share of Saunderson's Wines but also everything you had expected to inherit from my father. As my wife, you could continue to live here at Cuckmere Hall and enjoy the affluent lifestyle Ralph provided, until he named me as his heir.'

He smiled cynically when she shook her head. 'I'm not a fool, *querida*. I always practice safe sex. Perhaps you were out of your mind from whatever substance you had taken at your birthday party, but I'll prompt your memory and remind you that I used a condom. I'm afraid you will have to look elsewhere for a husband and a father for your child.'

Elin swayed on her feet, whether for dramatic effect or because she hadn't fully recovered from fainting a few minutes ago, Cortez did not know and he told himself he didn't care. She swallowed before she spoke. 'Only a fool would believe that contraception is one hundred per cent effective, and in our case it failed.'

She lifted her chin and met his gaze, and for some reason he was compelled to look away from her intense blue stare. 'Believe me, hell will freeze over before I'd ever want to marry you,' she said coldly. 'Harry is yours, but I might have known you would shirk your responsibility for your son when you scuttled off without even having the decency to say goodbye after you'd had sex with me.'

'You were in a deep sleep and I did not think you would appreciate me waking you,' he bit out, incensed by her scathing tone and her insistence on continuing with what was undoubtedly a lie. He did not believe for a minute that he was the father of her child. *Dios*, after what had happened with Alandra he had taken care never to have unprotected sex.

Even so, he disliked the image Elin had presented

of him hurrying out of her bedroom while she slept because he could not deny that was exactly what he'd done. He'd been rattled that she had made him lose control and he had left before he'd given in to the temptation to kiss her awake and make love to her again, slowly, taking his time to explore her beautiful body so that she gasped and moaned while he pleasured her.

Cortez swore silently as his body reacted predictably to his erotic thoughts, and he forced himself to focus on the present situation. He wasn't surprised that Elin had played the oldest trick in the book to try to secure financial security for herself, after she'd learned that she and her brother had been excluded almost entirely from their adoptive father's will. He could not imagine that 'the party princess'—as one of the tabloids had nicknamed her—had ever held down a job. She needed a source of income, but what was surprising was how quickly she conceded defeat.

'I've done my duty and informed you that you have a son,' she said crisply. 'I neither want nor expect anything from you, except for a few days' grace while I arrange to move out of Cuckmere Hall.' Her voice bore the faintest tremor and she pressed her lips together before she continued. 'You are aware that Ralph left my brother and I each a property on the estate. But the cottages have been empty for several years and I don't know what state they are in. I may need to have some renovation work done before I can take a baby to live there.'

He reminded himself that she did not deserve his compassion. She had enjoyed a privileged lifestyle, which had been denied to his mother and him when he was a child. But Ralph's vile treatment of his mother was nothing to do with Elin, Cortez conceded. Nor was it her fault that she had grown up in the gracious surroundings of Cuckmere Hall, while he had spent his boyhood working in the vineyards in the blazing Spanish sun, helping his mother to eke out a living.

'I'm going back to London to meet the board of Saunderson's Bank this afternoon,' he told her. 'I have no plans to return to Sussex for a week or so. You and your brother can remain at Cuckmere Hall while you make arrangements to move into the cottages Ralph left you.'

'I doubt Jarek will want to live in a cottage. He has his own home in London.' She hesitated. 'My brother had anticipated that he would become chairman of the bank. What will happen now? Will he continue in his current job?'

'For the immediate future the situation will remain unchanged, until I have met the board of directors. When I have assessed all aspects of the bank's business portfolio there are likely to be changes,' he warned. 'Ralph's will was as much of a surprise to me as it was to you. I was informed of his death by Mr Carstairs and I attended the funeral to pay my respects to my father, even though he had never given my mother the respect she deserved.'

Cortez did not try to disguise his bitterness. His mother had been an angel and his greatest regret was that she had died before he'd become rich and successful and he hadn't had the chance to make her life more comfortable.

'It was a great shock to discover that my adoptive father had a secret son,' Elin said quietly. 'How did your mother meet Ralph?'

'She worked as a maid here at Cuckmere Hall. My mother never spoke of my father or revealed his identity and I had no idea that I was Ralph's son until I received a request for a DNA test. When I met Ralph he explained that he'd had an affair with my mother at the same time as he became engaged to Lorna Amhurst. He said his marriage was an arrangement to merge two banking families.'

Cortez frowned. 'Ralph insisted that he gave my mother money when she told him she was pregnant. He assumed she returned to her family in Spain. But her family threw her out for having an illegitimate child and she brought me up on her own, with no money other than the small income she earned from growing grapes used for making sherry.

'I don't know why Ralph made me his heir, but I think it is unlikely that he wanted to make amends for abandoning me before I was born,' he said cynically. 'A more obvious reason is that, having ignored me—his biological son—for most of my life, Ralph was faced with leaving his personal fortune and Saunderson's Bank to the mercy of his two adopted children who, despite the privileges of wealth and excellent education, have become spoiled brats in adulthood.'

Elin jerked her head back as if he had slapped her. *Dios*, how did this woman manage to make him feel as if he were a monster? Cortez thought frustratedly.

'You know nothing about me or my brother,' she said in a clipped voice that made him want to ruffle her cool composure and reveal the fire that he knew simmered beneath her air of refinement. 'Jarek is a thousand times a better man than you could ever be.'

Finally he glimpsed a flicker of emotion on her face that up until now had been a serene mask. It was interesting that her brother was her weak spot, he mused. Everyone had an Achilles heel and he had made it his particular line of expertise to detect weaknesses in an opponent which he could ruthlessly use to his advantage. Although he was unlikely to ever need to use boardroom tactics with Elin. She did not have anything he wanted—apart from the face of an angel and a body that would tempt the most devout saint to sin, he thought with grim humour.

But she was off limits. He'd had his share of one-night stands and saw nothing wrong for two consenting adults to enjoy sex without the complication of emotions. What he found intolerable was that Elin was the only woman he had been unable to forget. And yes, he'd tried the obvious method of having sex with other women, but after a few unsatisfactory encounters he hadn't had a mistress for months.

The dull ache in his groin mocked his belief that he'd lost interest in sex but, far from feeling relieved at the proof that his libido was functioning normally, he was consumed with equal measures of rage and a terrible hunger that he feared would be his doom. That *she* would be his doom.

Santa Madre. Cortez cursed beneath his breath and jerked his eyes from her lovely face and that soft mouth that he longed to taste. He glanced at his watch and realised he had already wasted too much time. Elin was a dangerous distraction. 'My meeting with the board of Saunderson's Bank is scheduled for three o'clock, and I need to leave now if I am to make it on time.'

He walked over to the door and paused to glance back at her. 'I will make arrangements for a representative from a hotel design company to visit Cuckmere Hall next week. They should not inconvenience you while you are packing to move out.'

'Hotel?' she said sharply. 'You…you're not thinking of turning the house into a hotel?'

'It's one option I am considering. I have no desire to live in an ugly Gothic monstrosity.' He strode into the hall and Elin followed him.

'Cuckmere isn't ugly. Admittedly the house is a quirky mix of architectural styles, but most of the main house was built or renovated in the early nineteenth century. There has been a house on this site since Tudor times and the Saunderson family have lived here since then. You are a Saunderson. Cuckmere Hall is your heritage…and…it is also your son's.'

Cortez could not control the fierce emotions that ripped through him at Elin's words. His mind flew back to when he had been in his early twenties and had moved to Madrid to start his career with Hernandez Bank. Life in the big city had been exciting, and when he'd met a stunning model, Alandra Ruiz, he'd fallen hard for her exotic looks.

He pictured himself in the bathroom of Alandra's apartment, staring at a pregnancy test he'd found on the vanity unit. He'd picked up the test and carried it into the bedroom.

'When were you going to tell me you are pregnant, *carina*?'

Her reaction had surprised him. She had frowned and then given a careless shrug. 'I meant to throw the test away before you saw it.'

'So it's true—you're going to have my baby?' He'd never felt so happy in his life. The woman he loved was pregnant with his child, and he was filled with excitement and pride.

But Alandra had pushed him away when he'd tried to take her in his arms. 'Don't be ridiculous. I can't go through with the pregnancy,' she'd snapped. 'For one thing, getting fat will ruin my career. But, more importantly, Emilio will know it is not his child because he has been abroad for months.'

Cortez had felt as though a lead weight had dropped into his stomach. 'Who the hell is Emilio?'

'He's my fiancé.' Alandra gave another shrug. 'He has moved to Canada, where he has a good job, and I'm waiting for a visa so that I can join him in Toronto. I was bored and you were a little light entertainment,' she'd told Cortez. 'But it has to end now.'

He had tried to persuade her to keep the baby. 'Marry me and I'll take care of you and our child,' he'd begged.

At first she had laughed at him. 'You don't earn half as much as Emilio, and I don't want his baby, so why would I want yours?' Eventually she had agreed, and he had been overjoyed, but days later Alandra had called him and said she had never been serious about accepting his proposal and she had got rid of his baby before flying to Canada to be with her fiancé.

Cortez snapped his thoughts back to the present. Elin had to be lying because if she'd really had his child why wouldn't she have told him before now and demanded money? Alandra had ripped his heart out when she'd got rid of his baby, and he refused to give credence to the idea that he could be the father of Elin's child when the chances were frankly negligible.

'I don't have a son,' he snapped. He swung away from her and moved towards the front door, but she came after him and put her hand on his arm.

'Please, Cortez…'

Please, Cortez. He pictured her sprawled on a bed

with her scarlet dress awry. He heard her soft voice urging him on, inciting his hunger, his desperation to sink between her soft white thighs. She had made him feel out of control a year ago and she was threatening his self-control now. He wanted to haul her back to the sofa in the library and slide her elegant black dress up to her waist to bare her to his hungry gaze. He wanted her more than he'd ever wanted any other woman, and his need infuriated him and at a deeper level it shamed him. Cortez Ramos did not *need* anyone. Certainly not a social butterfly who, if only half the press stories about her were true, was a trollop.

He stared at her hand on his arm while the silence in the hall simmered with tension. She was standing so close that he breathed in her perfume, a light floral fragrance with underlying sensual notes of jasmine, and the beast inside him roared. He brought his other hand up and snapped his fingers around her wrist to jerk it away from his arm.

'If you ever repeat your unfounded accusation that I am the father of your child I will sue you for slander,' he said grimly. 'We had protected sex on one occasion. It would be *too* convenient from your point of view if you had conceived my child, but I don't believe you did.'

He pulled open the front door and the cold March air stung his nostrils as he dragged in a breath. 'It is not wise to play games with me, Elin. Unlike you, I did not enjoy a privileged upbringing. When I was a boy my mother often could not afford to buy food for us, but the hunger in my belly fired my determination to succeed and escape the poverty of my childhood. I've heard that Ralph Saunderson had a reputation for being ruthless and, I warn you, in that respect I take after my father.'

CHAPTER FOUR

ELIN WATCHED CORTEZ ease his tall frame into the low-slung sports car parked on the drive and slammed the front door shut as if she were shutting out the devil. She released her breath on a shuddering sigh and leaned against the solid wooden door for support while she replayed the unbelievable scene in the library over in her mind.

She did not know what was most shocking: Ralph's will which stipulated that she must marry before she could claim her inheritance, or that Ralph's natural son and heir was Cortez Ramos—the father of her baby son, who had been conceived as a result of her night of shame.

Harry was the innocent one in all of this. With a low cry, she ran across the hall and up the sweeping staircase. Her suite of rooms, including the nursery, were in the east wing of the house. Cuckmere Hall had been her home since she was four years old and the possibility that Cortez might turn it into a hotel felt like another stab of a knife into her already mortally wounded heart.

The sound of her son's cries drove every other thought from her mind as she flew across the nursery and lifted him out of his cot. 'It's all right, sweetheart. Mummy's here,' she crooned softly, feeling a familiar clench of emotion when Harry buried his face in her neck and his cries subsided to little snuffles.

'I was just preparing his next feed,' the nanny explained, hurrying into the room from the private kitchen. 'Do you want me to give it to him?'

'No, I will.' Elin held out her hand for the bottle of formula and quashed a flicker of jealousy of the nanny. Barbara Lennox had proved to be invaluable and she had also become a trusted friend.

Elin had not planned to hire a nanny. But she had been desperately ill after giving birth to Harry and when she had finally left hospital and returned to Cuckmere Hall with her newborn son, Jarek had told her that he had employed Barbara temporarily while Elin regained her strength. Suffering a life-threatening haemorrhage moments after the birth had been a terrifying ordeal and, despite having been given two blood transfusions, she'd still felt weak and exhausted. To make matters worse, she'd then developed a serious kidney infection and had been too ill to be able to take care of her baby.

Barbara had turned down another job offer to stay and help look after Harry. It occurred to Elin that she would no longer be able to afford to employ a nanny now that Ralph had left her nothing in his will.

She hadn't felt a sense of entitlement, as Cortez had implied, but for twenty-two years she had regarded Ralph as her father and she was deeply hurt by the evidence that he had not cared about her.

She settled herself in a chair and felt a pang of guilt when Harry nuzzled his face against her breast and tried to suckle. 'Here you are,' she murmured, offering him the teat of the bottle. It was a lasting sadness that she had been unable to breastfeed him because of the strong antibiotics she'd had to take to fight the kidney infection, but Barbara had assured her that Harry was thriving on formula milk.

He was now just over three months old and he had a surprisingly strong grip when he curled his chubby fist around her finger. She couldn't resist kissing his downy cheek and silky black hair. He stared up at her with his big eyes that were already changing from dark blue to an even darker brown flecked with gold that reminded her of Cortez's eyes.

She could insist on a DNA test to prove that Cortez was Harry's father, but what would be the point? she thought wearily. Cortez did not want his son and she would not demean herself by pursuing him through the courts for a maintenance pay-out. Harry was her responsibility and she was prepared to bring him up on her own. At least she would have somewhere for them to live. Rose and Ivy Cottages were tucked away on a remote part of the Cuckmere estate. She knew Jarek would insist she took ownership of whichever cottage was in the best condition. He rarely came to east Sussex and when he was in England he stayed at his London penthouse apartment, but most of the time he lived in Japan, where he worked as head derivatives trader for Saunderson's Bank.

She would have to look for another job. Elin chewed on her lower lip as the harsh reality of her situation sank in. Marriage was not an option. She did not have a prospective husband handily available and, even if she could bear to force herself onto the dating scene, she was a single parent with no money or prospects and she was hardly a great catch. But it meant that under the terms of Ralph's will Cortez would inherit one hundred per cent of Saunderson's Wines.

The pain that had lodged beneath her breastbone following her mother's death gave a sharp tug with the realisation that she would not be able to fulfil Lorna Saunderson's dream of producing a top quality English wine from Cuckmere's vineyards that Lorna herself had planted.

It was conceivable that Cortez would allow her to continue in her role as production manager of the winery, but she did not relish the thought of working for him. Not if there was a chance she might see him regularly. She could not risk it when he had such a powerful effect on her. She pictured his handsome face: the chiselled cheekbones and square jaw, those dark, almost black eyes with their golden flecks and his wickedly sensual mouth that promised heaven— and delivered. Oh, boy, did it deliver.

Memories she'd blanked out for over a year filled

her mind. His lips on hers, the way he had plundered her soul and ravished her senses with his devastating kiss. Until today she'd convinced herself that her outrageous behaviour on the night of her birthday party had been the result of her drink being spiked with a date-rape drug by one of the other guests. But when she had seen Cortez in the library at the reading of Ralph's will, her body had betrayed her and forced her to acknowledge the shameful truth. She had fallen into bed with him a year ago because she'd seen him across a crowded room and she'd wanted him so badly it had *hurt*.

She had ignored the voice in her head which warned her that a man as lethally attractive as him was way out of her league. He had stolen her breath and her sanity and all that had been left of her was a burning need to feel his arms around her, his mouth against her mouth, his body on her body. Damning memories of having sex with Cortez came storming back and her treacherous body betrayed her all over again. Her nipples tightened and the quiver she felt low in her stomach was a shameful reminder that she had behaved like a slut at her birthday party.

But her night of shame had resulted in her son. Harry finished his bottle and Elin held him against her shoulder while she winded him. Her heart turned over when he gave her a gummy smile. She would never regret having him even though she regretted the circumstances of his conception. She loved him so much and she vowed that as he grew up she would protect her son from the painful truth that his father had refused to acknowledge him.

She told herself it would be best if she forgot that Cortez Ramos existed but, after she had changed Harry's nappy and settled him in his cot, she found herself in front of her computer searching for Cortez's profile on social media sites. His biography revealed that he had spent his childhood living with his mother on a small vineyard in Andalucía. After graduating from university with a first-class business degree he had worked for one of Spain's largest banks and quickly proved he was a brilliant financier. His rise through the ranks to the position of CEO of Hernandez Bank had been meteoric.

It was no wonder that Ralph had chosen his illegitimate son to be chairman of Saunderson's Bank over his adopted son, Elin thought heavily. Ralph had been concerned that Jarek was too much of a risk-taker and it was an opinion shared by many of the board of directors, who would no doubt be very happy to have Cortez as the head of the bank.

His success was not confined to banking. He had earned a reputation as a skilled viticulturist, and at his vineyards and bodega near the town of Jerez de la Frontera he specialised in producing exceptionally fine sherry. Five years ago, Cortez had formed a partnership with an international sherry company to produce and export specialist sherries around the world. The business, Felipe & Cortez, had become so successful that he was reputedly a multimillionaire.

Elin was deep in thought as she switched off the computer. Her mind went blank for a moment when her phone rang and she answered a call from a catering company who wanted to discuss arrangements for the party that was to take place at Cuckmere Hall.

'Oh, yes, the event is definitely going ahead,' she confirmed to the caterers. The party was to raise funds for a charity organisation that she, Jarek and Ralph had established after Lorna Saunderson's death. Lorna's Gift aimed to support children living in orphanages around the world, and the many celebrities who had been invited to the party were likely to make huge donations to the charity.

Elin was sure her adoptive father would have wanted her to hold the party. But Cortez was now the owner of Cuckmere Hall and she did not have time to find another suitable venue. He had told her before he'd left for his business meeting in London that he did not plan to return to Sussex for some time. There was a good chance he would never find out that the party had taken place. Her conscience felt uncomfortable, but she reminded herself that the charity was already making a difference to the lives of orphaned children and it might be her last chance to hold a major fund-raising event before she had to leave Cuckmere Hall.

What if Elin had told him the truth?

The question had haunted Cortez when he'd driven away from Cuckmere Hall, and uncertainty had continued to plague him for the past two days while he'd had meetings with the board and management team of Saunderson's Bank. He had dismissed Elin's claim that he was the father of her child because he was ninety-nine per cent certain she was lying. But that left a one per cent possibility that it was true.

His conscience pricked that he had rejected her claim outright and rushed away from Cuckmere because he hadn't trusted himself around her. She unsettled him in a way no other woman had ever done and he resented the effect she had on him. But he needed to rule out the slim chance he had a son, which was why, instead of spending a relaxing evening at the house in Kensington, he had driven down the motorway back to Sussex in the pouring rain that at times had turned to sleet.

Cuckmere Hall was a beacon of blazing lights against the black sky. When Cortez turned the car through the gates of the estate he was surprised to see dozens of vehicles parked on the driveway in front of the house. He was tired, which was perhaps understandable after the bizarre last few days, when he'd learned that the man he struggled to think of as his father had bequeathed him the chairmanship of the UK's most prestigious private bank. The role came with a huge amount of responsibility and the expectation of the board that the bank would flourish under his leadership. But he felt no loyalty to Ralph Saunderson, who had ignored him for thirty-four years and had only made Cortez his heir because Ralph's adopted son was not up to the job of running Saunderson's Bank.

The journey from London and the foul English weather had darkened Cortez's mood even more, and his temper simmered when he walked into Cuckmere Hall and found a party going on. He threaded his way through the crowd of people in the central hall and shook his head at the waiter who offered him a tray of canapés. In one of the reception rooms there was a champagne bar, and in the ballroom music blared from the speakers and people were dancing.

He saw Elin immediately, and the punch in his gut made him catch his breath. It was history repeating itself, he thought furiously. She was even wearing a red dress like she had done at her birthday party a year ago. But, instead of a scrap of scarlet silk, her dress tonight was a burgundy velvet floor-length gown with a side split up to her mid-thigh. The top of the dress was strapless, leaving her shoulders bare, and the laced bodice pushed her breasts up so that they looked like ripe, round peaches that he longed to taste. Her pale blonde hair reached to halfway down her back and shimmered like raw silk.

He wanted her. *Dios*, he could feel the thunder of his pulse, and the fire in his blood mocked his belief that his desire for her a year ago had been an aberration. What was it about Elin that tested his self-control to its limits? She was not the only beautiful woman he had known, not even the most beautiful—

her eyes were too big in her heart-shaped face and her mouth was too wide. She was elfin and ethereal and too petite for his six feet four frame.

The rage inside him turned darker and more dangerous as he watched her dancing with a man he vaguely recognised was a television chat show host. The guy's hands were all over Elin, but she seemed to be enjoying the attention, and her lilting laughter audible above the music caused acid to fizz in Cortez's gut. He snapped his teeth together and strode across the ballroom, driven to distraction by an unfamiliar emotion that he grimly realised was jealousy.

'My turn, I think you'll find,' he growled to Elin's dance partner. The other man obviously valued his doubtless exorbitantly expensive dental work and quickly dropped his hand from her waist.

'That was incredibly rude.' Elin threw Cortez a furious glare before she spun round and began to walk away, but he snaked his arm around her waist and jerked her towards him.

'I'm sure you don't want to cause a scene, so I suggest you dance with me.'

'*I'm* not the one causing a scene,' she snapped. 'Do you know who that man is? He is Clint Cooper, one of the highest paid people on television, and he was about to promise me a lot of money before you barged him out of the way.'

'*Santa Madre*, you would barter yourself like a whore on a street corner?' Cortez made no effort to hide his disgust, but to his fury he realised that he still wanted her and he didn't care that she had lived up to her reputation in the tabloids as a goodtime girl.

'How dare you?' She reacted instantly and swung her hand up, but his reactions were quicker and he seized her wrist before she could slap his cheek.

'Careful,' he warned her softly. 'If you hit me, I'll retaliate. Right here in front of your guests, I will put you across my knee and spank you as befits the spoiled brat you are. And, believe me, I would dare, Elin.'

The pink flush on her cheeks deepened to scarlet and she breathed jerkily, causing her breasts to quiver above the low-cut neckline of her dress. Her eyes flashed with temper, but Cortez sensed the scorching sexual chemistry beneath her anger and he felt an answering lick of fire along his manhood.

'You are an odious man,' she hissed. 'Why are you even here? You said you would be staying in London.'

'Is that why you decided to throw a party while I was conveniently out of the way? I'm sure I don't have to remind you that Ralph left me Cuckmere Hall. The house and estate are mine by right of birth—even though my father failed to acknowledge me for most of my life.' He could not hide his bitterness. 'I suppose you are angry because your adoptive father excluded you from his will, but I find it distasteful that you arranged a party two days after Ralph's funeral. You might as well have danced on his grave.'

She stiffened when he moved his hand to the small of her back and held her tightly against him so that she was forced to dance with him. 'As a matter of fact, Ralph helped to organise the party before he died,' she snapped. 'The charity, Lorna's Gift, was my brother's idea and all the funds raised go to helping children living in orphanages around the world.'

She pointed to a banner on the wall that he had not noticed because his attention had been riveted on Elin. The banner had the slogan *Lorna's Gift* and a photograph of a sweet-faced woman who he guessed was Lorna Saunderson. Cortez was aware that Ralph's wife had died eighteen months ago.

'Clint Cooper was telling me of his intention to make a donation to the charity,' Elin continued furiously. 'He was not offering me money for sex. What gives you the right to judge me?' Her mouth trembled and Cortez sensed she was struggling to control her emotions. 'Do you think I don't judge myself?' she said in a low voice. 'My birthday party a year ago was the most shameful night of my life. You have no idea how bitterly I regret that I had sex with you.'

Cortez told himself she was a good actress. He *knew* her air of innocence was fake. He focused his thoughts on the reason he had driven from London to Sussex on a filthy night. 'I need to talk to you, but not in here with this deafening music.' He had noticed there was a conservatory next to the ballroom and he steered her over to it. The glass room was empty and he closed the door to muffle the sound of the disco.

Elin immediately stepped away from him and put her hands on her hips. 'What now?' she demanded belligerently. 'After we spoke two days ago I got the impression that you had nothing more to say to me, and I certainly have nothing to say to you.'

He pushed away the infuriating thought that she looked magnificent when she was angry. Her blue eyes gleamed with the fiery brilliance of sapphires and her breasts heaved beneath her velvet gown. 'When was your son born?' he said abruptly.

'The sixth of October.' She did not drop her gaze from his, and Cortez narrowed his eyes to hide his inexplicable feeling of disappointment.

'So he is five months old. You could at least have worked out the maths. You must have conceived in January last year, but we had sex in March.' His lip curled in disgust as another thought occurred to him. '*Dios*. You must have been pregnant when you slept with me, but you told me I was responsible. Surely you had the sense to realise I would not accept a paternity claim without a DNA test?'

She shrugged. 'It was worth a try.'

Dark and dangerous emotions swirled inside him and he felt the same savage wrench in his gut that he'd felt years ago when Alandra had informed him that she had terminated her pregnancy. He had wanted his baby but he hadn't been given a chance to be a father. Tonight he had come to Cuckmere Hall because he'd realised there was a chance he was the father of Elin's son. But she had lied and made a clumsy attempt to foist another man's child on him.

His jaw clenched as he struggled to control his anger. He was furious, not only with Elin but with himself because, despite the proof that she was a lying bitch, he was trapped in her spell and the shaming hunger he felt for her was a weakness he found intolerable.

'I warned you not to play games with me.' He resisted the urge to shake some sense into her. If he touched her he feared he would be lost. 'Maybe your whole life is a game of endless parties and various sexual partners, but you have a child to consider. I know what it is like to grow up without a father. What will you tell your son when he asks why he doesn't have a father?'

She paled, and that made him even angrier. How dare she look so *tragic*, as if he had wounded her, when he knew—when everyone who read the English tabloids knew about her wild sex-and-drugs party girl reputation?

'I'll tell Harry the truth,' she said quietly, 'which is that his father did not want him.' Her voice hardened. 'You're such a hypocrite. You think that it's fine for you to sleep around, but you judge the women you sleep with. That's blatant double standards. Equality between the sexes means nothing.

It's still women who are left with the babies when they are abandoned by their lovers.'

Elin stalked out of the conservatory without giving Cortez a chance to reply. She was incensed by his arrogance and reassured herself that she had done the right thing by misleading him about Harry's date of birth. Cortez had made it clear he did not want a child, and after hearing his insulting opinion of her it was impossible to see how they could both have a role in Harry's life.

It was equally impossible to understand why she allowed herself to be affected by Cortez. But she did not allow it, she thought bitterly. She was kidding herself if she believed she had any control over her reaction to his dangerous good looks, and that *thing* that smouldered between them, that intense heat that licked through her veins every time she met his gaze and saw the gold flecks in his dark eyes blaze. She did not know what she found more unsettling—her uncontrollable fascination with him, or the realisation that he desired her, and despised himself for it.

The din in the ballroom, of guests talking loudly in competition with the blaring disco music, had given Elin a headache and after her run-in with Cortez she felt an urgent need to be with her baby. But as she exited the ballroom and was about to run upstairs to the nursery, someone called her name.

'Nat!' She smiled at the young man who hurried over to her. Nat Davies drove a tractor at the vineyard and he also worked in the winery where his father, Stan, was head winemaker for Saunderson's Wines. 'Are you enjoying the party?'

'Yeah, it's great. But Dad's just called me and said there's a problem at the vineyard.'

Elin frowned as Nat went on to explain that the latest weather forecast predicted an overnight frost. 'There are already buds on the vines after that unusually warm spell we had at the beginning of March,' he reminded her. 'Frost damage now could ruin the entire crop.'

It could mean the end of Lorna Saunderson's dream of producing a top quality sparkling wine in England that was on a par with wines from across the Channel. Elin remembered how ten years ago Mama had been inspired to establish a vineyard in Sussex after visiting the Champagne region of France. Ralph had initially been enthusiastic but, as was his way, he had quickly lost interest in the project. It had been Lorna and Elin, aided by a small team of estate workers, who had planted fifteen acres of Chardonnay and Pinot Noir vines in the chalky soil.

The winery had been producing wine for seven years, and the previous year's vintage had been the best yet. Following Lorna's death, it had been important to Elin to keep her mother's dream alive, but the terms of Ralph's will meant that her involvement with Saunderson's Wines would soon be over. The vines were Cortez's responsibility now, she reminded herself. But she couldn't bear the idea that all the years of Mama's hard work could be wiped out by a frost.

'We'll have to light the frost candles,' she told Nat. She glanced at her watch. 'It's almost midnight. We need to hurry before the temperature drops to below freezing. Go and round up any of the estate workers from the party who are sober enough to help.'

Twenty minutes later, Elin drove the farm truck through the grounds of the Cuckmere estate up to the vineyard. It was a clear night and the full moon cast a silver gleam over the rolling Sussex Downs. She briefly wondered what Cortez would make of her if he saw her as she was dressed now. She had changed out of her glamorous ball gown, into jeans and as many jumpers as she could fit beneath her duffel coat.

The air was icy when she climbed out of the truck and walked through the vineyard, but remembering her last conversation with Cortez made her burn with anger. She had not noticed his car on the drive, and hoped he had returned to London and she would never see him again. It was imperative that she moved out of Cuckmere Hall as soon as possible so that she could avoid him. Although it would break her heart to leave the only home she had ever known, she thought bleakly.

She forced her mind away from Cortez Ramos and concentrated on the task of lighting eight hundred *bougies*—or frost candles. They were the size of big paint tins, filled with paraffin wax and a wick, and were placed at intervals between the rows of vines. When the *bougies* were lit they warmed the air temperature enough to prevent frost from damaging the tender new shoots on the plants.

It was laborious work walking along the endless rows of vines and stooping every few yards to light the candles, and Elin was grateful to Nat and his father and a couple of estate workers who had come to help. When they had finished, the sight of acres of vineyards glowing with golden lights was spectacular, but Elin knew that in a few hours all the candles would have to be extinguished when the sun rose and the temperature lifted a few degrees. She sent Nat and the other workers home, but Stan stayed with her to keep a watch on the *bougies*. It was nearly seven a.m. by the time they had put all the candles out and she was able to return to the house.

Harry was awake in his cot and greeted her with a winsome smile that melted her heart. While she fed him she had to force her eyes to remain open, until Barbara gently lifted the baby out of her arms. 'Go to bed for a couple of hours,' the nanny told her. 'I'll put Harry in his pram and take him for a walk. You won't be able to take care of him while you're exhausted from lack of sleep.'

Elin was too tired to argue but, when she crawled into bed, worries about the future circled in her mind. How would she manage to hold down a job and take care of her son without Barbara's help? What job was she likely to find when her only qualifications were in viticulture and oenology? Wine production was a growing industry in England but most vineyards were small, family run businesses.

There was also the question of where she was going to live. She had checked out the two cottages that Ralph had left her and her brother and found that both properties had a problem with damp, which would not be a healthy environment for a baby.

She had not heard from Jarek and he hadn't answered any of her calls. She hoped he hadn't been drinking too much. It was vital Cortez did not find out that her brother had developed a reliance on vodka to help him cope with his feelings of guilt and grief about Mama's death.

Elin's head felt as if it would explode, and when she did eventually fall asleep her shamefully erotic dreams were fuelled by memories of Cortez's naked, powerfully muscular body pressing down on her and the bold thrust of his manhood pushing between her thighs.

CHAPTER FIVE

THE GRAVEL CRUNCHED beneath Cortez's feet as he strode down the driveway. When he passed the ornamental pool he noticed there was a layer of ice on the surface of the water, despite the fact that it was officially the first day of spring. He missed the warmth and sunshine of southern Spain, and he'd told Elin the truth when he'd said he had no desire to live in the draughty monstrosity Cuckmere Hall which Ralph Saunderson had bequeathed to him.

He had left his car next to the gatehouse the previous night. There had been nowhere to park in front of the house because Elin's party guests had parked their cars there. This morning the only other vehicle on the driveway was an old truck that he assumed belonged to one of the estate workers. It was unlikely that the party princess would drive a mud-spattered farm vehicle, Cortez thought cynically.

He recalled his sleepless night in the master bedroom which the staff had prepared for him. The past few days had been hectic, and he'd been unable to face driving back to London late at night. But it had felt strange to be in the room that had once been Ralph Saunderson's. He'd wondered if his father had invited his mother into the bedroom when she had been employed at the house as a maid. It had occurred to Cortez that in all probability he had been conceived at Cuckmere Hall, but when his mother had revealed she was pregnant Ralph had sent her back to Spain. He frowned as he remembered the remark Elin had made that women were in a vulnerable position if they were abandoned by their lover and left to bring up a baby alone. It was why he had visited Elin again, to establish if there was any chance he could be her baby's father.

Now he knew what a lying bitch she was, he thought savagely. He unlocked his car and threw his bag into the boot. The sound of a baby crying caught his attention and he looked up to see a woman dressed in a beige nurse's uniform pushing a pram down the driveway. He guessed she was the nanny and the crying infant must be Elin's son. Despite himself, Cortez was curious.

'Good morning.' He smiled at the woman. 'Your charge does not sound happy.'

She halted beside the car and gave a rueful laugh. 'I think Harry wants his mother but Miss Saunderson is sleeping in this morning.'

Cortez glanced into the pram and shock jolted through him when he saw that the baby had a mass of jet-black hair. He visualised Elin's pale blonde hair and doubt flickered in his mind. There was no way the child could be his because the date of conception did not tally with when he'd slept with Elin, he assured himself.

'At the party last night Elin mentioned that her son is five months old,' he said casually to the nanny.

'As a matter of fact he is three months.' The nanny reached into the pram and folded the blanket away from the baby's face. 'Although he is growing so fast that he could be mistaken as being older.'

'I must have misheard Elin. I thought she said her son was born in October,' Cortez murmured. He stared into the pram and was aware of the painful thud of his heart. The baby had ceased crying and stared back at him with unblinking dark eyes flecked with gold.

'Harry's birthday is the sixth of December,' the nanny told him. 'Elin says he was an early Christmas present.' She gave Cortez a polite nod before she continued to walk down the drive, pushing the pram in front of her. She did not appear to hear the choked sound he made as his acute sense of shock turned to anger.

Why had Elin lied about her baby's date of birth? *Could* black-haired, dark-eyed little Harry be his son? He would get the truth from Elin if he had to drag it out of her, Cortez vowed grimly.

The butler greeted him deferentially when he returned to the house. The staff had been informed that he was Ralph Saunderson's son and heir and no doubt they hoped to keep their jobs at Cuckmere Hall. He elicited from Baines that Elin's suite of rooms were in the east wing. He took the stairs two at a time and strode down the corridor, but when he hammered on the door there was no answer. Without hesitating he turned the handle and walked into a large sitting room.

The elegantly furnished room was filled with light that poured in through the tall windows overlooking the gardens at the back of the house. Cortez thought of the rundown farmhouse where he had lived with his mother when he was a boy. The house had only had two rooms and he'd slept on the couch in the living room. Many nights he had lain awake watching his mother sewing traditional flamenco dresses which she sold to tourists at the market as a way of earning a little more money.

Once again bitterness surged through him as he recalled the poverty he and his mother had endured while his father's adopted daughter had grown up in the luxurious surroundings of an English mansion. According to the nanny, Elin was still in bed at ten o'clock in the morning. No doubt she had enjoyed being the lady of the manor since Lorna Saunderson's death and had expected that her affluent lifestyle would continue. It must have been a great shock when she'd learned that Ralph had left her virtually nothing, Cortez thought cynically.

He prowled through the private suite of rooms and discovered a small kitchen and a nursery painted a sunny yellow. Something on the wall of the nursery caught Cortez's eye and he walked over to take a closer look at a framed photo of a newborn baby wearing a hospital tag on his wrist. The baby's birth weight and date of birth were printed beneath the photo, stating that Harry had entered the world on the sixth of December, weighing seven pounds and two ounces.

Cortez's jaw was rigid with tension as he knocked on the door next to the nursery. There was no reply and, unable to contain his impatience, he let himself into what was obviously Elin's bedroom. As he glanced around at the pastel pink décor a door at the far end of the room opened and Elin walked into her bedroom from the en suite bathroom.

She was naked and Cortez's breath rushed from his lungs as he was transfixed by the sight of her. The pale spring sunshine streaming through the window bathed her body in a pearlescent light so that she looked ethereal and so beautiful that he felt blinded, as if he had looked directly at the sun. Her fair hair cascaded down her back like a river of gold. She reminded him of a painting of the goddess Aphrodite with her alabaster skin and perfect, small round breasts tipped with rose. He moved his gaze over her flat stomach and narrow hips to the neat cluster of pale gold curls between her thighs, and he was so hard that his arousal was almost painful.

Time seemed to be suspended, but in reality only a few seconds could have passed before Elin snatched up her robe from the bed and wrapped it around her.

'What are you doing in here?' she demanded. 'You have no right to barge into my private rooms.'

Her face was flushed and Cortez had noticed before she'd covered her body with her robe that a pink stain had spread down her throat and over her breasts. The ability to blush at will was no doubt a useful tool in her armoury of feminine wiles, he thought cynically.

'Actually, I have the right to enter any room in *my* house,' he corrected her, struggling to bring his raging libido under control. 'I knocked but you can't have heard me.'

She crossed her arms over her chest, but not before he'd noticed the prominent outline of her nipples beneath her silk robe. The knowledge that she was as much at the mercy of their mutual desire as he was did not appease his grim mood.

'You said I could stay at Cuckmere Hall while I arrange to move into other accommodation,' she said stiffly. 'What do you want?'

'Why did you lie about your baby's date of birth? The nanny told me your son was born in December, not October as you told me.'

She shrugged. 'Why do you care?'

He crossed the room in a couple of strides to stand in front of her, and felt an unholy satisfaction when she shrank from him. Good, he wanted to rattle her. 'Tell me the truth, damn you.'

'How can I tell you the truth when you threatened to sue me for slander?' she snapped. 'Harry was born in December, nine months after we slept together. Work the maths out for yourself.'

'But that does not necessarily mean I am his father.' He refused to believe her claim without proof. 'You might have slept with other men at around the same time that you had sex with me. Statistically, the chance of a condom failing to be effective is very small.'

'You are the *only* man I've ever had sex with,' she said in a taut voice with an underlying note of hurt that Cortez dismissed with a sardonic laugh.

'Your pretence of innocence is ridiculous when details of your love-life are frequently reported by the gutter press.'

Elin drew a sharp breath as if he had struck her. But she quickly controlled the tremble of her soft mouth, and her blue eyes were clear and perhaps a little too bright when she lifted her head and met his gaze. 'Believe what you like. I don't give a damn what you think of me. But I'd appreciate it if you would get out of my room and at least have the decency to respect my privacy. I assure you I won't remain at Cuckmere for any longer than it takes me to find somewhere for me and Harry to live.'

'The only way to resolve the issue of the child's paternity is to have a DNA test. And if he *is* my son, you won't be taking him anywhere.'

'You can't stop me,' she flared. 'I'll deny you are his father. You made it clear that you don't want a child. It will be better for Harry to grow up knowing nothing about you than for him to discover that you didn't want him.'

'If you refuse to allow a DNA test I will apply to the court for the right to discover if I have a child.' He could not hide his frustration as he raked his hair off his brow and despised the hard clench his body gave when he breathed in her scent: sensual jasmine perfume and a fresh lemon fragrance in her hair. 'I never said I would not want my son,' he said gruffly. 'But I am suspicious that you are now backtracking your claim, perhaps because a paternity test will prove you are a liar.'

Cortez's anger simmered. He told himself it was because he wanted Elin to give him a straight answer, but deep down he acknowledged the far simpler truth was that he wanted *her*. He couldn't dismiss the image of her naked body from his mind, and knowing that her dove-grey silk robe was all that hid her slender beauty from his gaze was sending him quietly mad.

'If Harry is mine, why didn't you name me as his father when he was born?' he said abruptly.

She laughed, but it was not a happy laugh, it was cold and bitter, and the sound of it made something twist in his gut. 'How *could* I name you? I didn't know your full name, or anything about you.' She took him by surprise when she pushed past him. He followed her out of the bedroom and into the sitting room and watched her open a drawer in the bureau.

'This is Harry's birth certificate.' She handed him

the document and he noticed that a blank space had been left under the section headed 'Name and Surname of Father'. 'Do you have any idea how humiliated I felt when I registered his birth and I didn't know the name of my baby's father? All I knew was that I'd had sex with someone called Cortez, but how could I know you were in fact my adoptive father's real son? And as you didn't stick around the next morning I had no way of contacting you when I found out I was pregnant.'

Temper had turned her eyes to the deep, dark blue of an ocean. 'You blamed Ralph for treating your mother badly by abandoning her when she was pregnant, but your behaviour was even worse than your father's. You knew who I was, and you could easily have got in contact with me. But you didn't because I was just a one-night stand and you did not care about how I might be feeling, even though you must have realised when we had sex that it was my first time.'

Her words dropped into the room like a pebble thrown into a pool, shattering the calm surface and creating ripples. For a few seconds the effect on Cortez was just as shattering, before he remembered all those goddamned press stories about her busy love-life.

'What I have realised is that you are a fantasist,' he said grimly. 'You are also delusional if you think I'd believe you were a virgin after you had invited me into your bedroom and told me with that pretty mouth of yours that you wanted me. I can't deny it was convenient that you kept contraceptives in the bedside drawer, but the fact that you were prepared for sex suggests you'd had previous lovers.'

He shrugged. 'I don't judge you for being sexually active and I do not hold double standards, as you accused me. But I deplore lying, which is why I insist on a DNA test, which will prove if I am your baby's father or if your claim is another lie.'

Elin had turned so pale that he wondered if she was going to faint. Or was it another ploy designed to gain his sympathy? Cortez thought cynically.

'I've already explained that on the night of my birthday party my behaviour was affected by a drug that I was unaware I had taken,' she said with a quiet dignity that disturbed him more than it should have done. 'My drink had been spiked with a date-rape drug that made me unable to control my thoughts and reactions.'

Anger growled in his voice. 'Are you suggesting I slipped you a drug with the intention of sexually assaulting you?'

'No, I know it wasn't you who spiked my drink. But, all the same, it was the effects of the drug that led me to have sex with you.'

'Really?' He disguised his fury behind a mocking smile. 'So you're saying that if you hadn't been drugged you would not have wanted me to kiss you? I assume you are not under the influence of any kind of behaviour-altering drug now?'

She looked puzzled. 'Of course not.'

'Then let us put your theory to the test.' He reached for her and watched her eyes widen as she realised his intention. But, curiously, she did not try to evade him, or perhaps he was simply too quick as he pulled her into his arms and bent his head.

Her mouth was a sweet promise that had driven him to distraction and a sensual memory that had disturbed his dreams for too long. He covered her lips with his and kissed her with a hunger and need that should have appalled him if he had been able to think. But he was lost the instant she opened her mouth beneath his and allowed him to probe his tongue into her sweetness. Triumph surged through Cortez as he felt the tension ease from her body and she melted into him, soft against his hardness, her surrender a delicious victory that he was determined to savour.

It had been so long. That was the only thought in Elin's mind as Cortez claimed her mouth with bold confidence and kissed her with devastating passion. It was more than a year since she had been in his arms, but it felt like a lifetime of loneliness, waiting for him, dreaming of him, secretly yearning for him. Now he was here, as dark and dangerously attractive as she remembered him, and she was incapable of resisting his mastery. Her traitorous body melted with the first brush of his lips against hers, and when he deepened the kiss and demanded her response the fire inside her became an inferno.

He drew her closer to him, crushing her against his whipcord body and making her aware of his strength and his desire. His arousal jabbed between her thighs, and with a low moan she stood on tiptoe so that she could press her pelvis against the hard bulge outlined beneath his jeans. He muttered something incomprehensible as he clamped his hand on her bottom, and when he kissed her again he thrust his tongue into her mouth in an erotic mimicry of sex.

The kiss went on and on and she never wanted it to end. There was nothing but heat and flame and searing need. Hers. His. Whatever Cortez might think of her, the potent force of his arousal betrayed his hunger.

She was stunned when he released her and dropped his hands to his sides. Nothing made sense, not the thunder of her pulse, or the grim fury on his beautiful face, or the voice from the doorway.

'I do beg your pardon,' the nanny murmured, sounding embarrassed, before she stepped back into the corridor and closed the sitting room door behind her.

Barbara's timely interruption had been a godsend, Elin told herself as her memory stormed back and brought with it the humiliating knowledge that Cortez had kissed her to prove a point. She stared at him because she could not help herself. Because he was a sorcerer and she was trapped in his spell. She braced herself for his taunts. Dear heaven, after the way she'd responded to his kiss he probably thought she was a nymphomaniac. But, to her surprise, he broke eye contact first and she had an odd feeling that he was as shocked as she was by the tumultuous intensity of that kiss.

'We will take Harry to London today to have the DNA test carried out at a clinic which provides an express paternity testing service,' he said abruptly. 'I've booked us an appointment, and they promise to have the result within eight hours of the test. How soon can you be ready to leave?'

Elin realised it would be pointless to refuse the paternity test when Cortez had stated he would go to court to force her to agree. But she was infuriated by his arrogant belief that if he ordered her to jump she would ask how high. She had dozed for an hour this morning and woken with a headache, the result, no doubt, of her sleepless night. It was likely her shivery feeling was due to her getting so cold in the vineyard last night, she assured herself. The frost candles might have protected the vines but it had taken hours for her to warm up after her moonlit vigil. She dismissed her concern that she could be developing another kidney infection, which had been a recurrent problem since she'd given birth to Harry.

'Why are you in such a rush for the test? Three days ago you refused to consider the possibility that you could be Harry's father. I've told you I won't make any financial demands on you and you can just walk away and forget about the night we spent together, as I had pretty much done until you turned up at Cuckmere Hall.'

'You did not appear to have forgotten me when I kissed you just now,' he said sardonically.

She felt heat bloom on her face and silently cursed her fair skin that blushed so easily.

Cortez swung his gaze to the bureau where she kept Harry's birth certificate. He picked up the two passports that were lying in the drawer and studied them. 'Were you planning to take Harry abroad as you have a passport for him?'

'I've been invited to my friend's wedding in Rhodes and I had to apply for a passport for Harry so that I can take him abroad.' She frowned. 'When I met you at my birthday party I assumed you were one of Virginia's friends.'

He slipped both passports into his pocket. 'We'll take these to London with us. The DNA clinic might need to see them for identity verification. Do you know your brother's whereabouts?'

Elin had been about to demand that he give her the passports, but she was distracted by his question.

'Jarek should have returned to Saunderson's Bank in Japan,' Cortez continued. 'But I have been informed by the bank's manager that he failed to turn up for work.'

'I'm sure there's a good reason,' she said quickly. 'Perhaps his flight from England was delayed.' Elin silently acknowledged a more likely explanation was that Jarek had been on a drinking binge and was holed up in his London apartment in one of his black moods. But she was certainly not going to tell Cortez of her suspicion. However, it was vital that she went to London to try and talk some sense into her brother before he was sacked from his job.

'I suppose it makes sense to have the DNA test as soon as possible,' she said. 'I can be ready to leave in an hour.'

Cortez gave her a speculative look but fortunately he did not ask why she had suddenly changed her mind. 'Make it half an hour,' was all he said as he walked over to the door.

Truly he was the most self-centred man she'd ever met. She was tempted to wipe that smug look from his face before she remembered his threat last night when she had been goaded beyond endurance and had tried to slap him. To her eternal shame, an image came into her mind of being held across his knee while he administered a spanking, and the warmth that flared on her face was almost as hot as the molten sensation pooling between her legs.

Elin was shocked by the intensity of her sexual arousal. It had taken her body many weeks to recover from giving birth, and the effort of looking after a baby, the night feeds, lack of sleep and a fog of hormones clouding her brain meant that sex simply had not been on her radar. But one look at Cortez and it was all she could think about. She realised he was giving her an odd look and prayed he could not read her mind.

'You've obviously never had anything to do with babies,' she muttered. 'Taking a small child anywhere with all the paraphernalia they need is like a military operation.'

His dark eyes bored into her. 'I haven't witnessed you taking care of your son on either of my visits to Cuckmere Hall. Maybe you find motherhood boring compared to your exciting social life. It seems to me that you leave Harry with his nanny most of the time.'

Forty-five minutes later, Elin was still seething over Cortez's comments when he drove them to London in his car. During the journey she maintained a frosty silence and he seemed preoccupied with his own thoughts. The nanny, who was sitting in the back of the car next to Harry in his baby seat, made a couple of attempts at conversation but soon gave up.

Elin had asked Barbara to accompany them to London, thinking she might need the nanny to look after Harry while she searched for her brother in the bars near to his home in Notting Hill, where he was a regular customer. She was relieved when she received a text message from Jarek saying he was on a flight to Japan. It was one thing less to worry about. She suggested that Barbara might like to take the afternoon off to visit her daughter who lived in Greenwich. Cortez pulled over outside a Tube station to drop Barbara off, before driving on to the private clinic in central London.

It did not take long for the samples to be collected which would be analysed for the DNA test, and afterwards they drove to the townhouse in Kensington. Cortez had decreed that they would stay in London overnight while they waited for the result of the paternity test.

Walking into the house, Elin was swamped by memories of when she had slept with Cortez on her birthday a year ago. She was agonisingly aware of him as he carried Harry in his baby seat from the car. Her lips felt tender from where he had kissed her earlier, and when she flicked her tongue over them she could still taste him.

She was glad when he opened his laptop and told her that he intended to get on with some work. Her head was pounding, and although Harry was usually a placid baby he was fretful all afternoon and she couldn't settle him. As she paced up and down the nursery with the inconsolable baby in her arms she decided that she must be a bad mother, as Cortez had implied.

'Why does he keep crying?' Cortez asked when he walked into the kitchen and found her struggling to make up a bottle of baby formula with one hand while she jiggled Harry on her hip. 'Could he be ill?'

'He's just a bit colicky. Babies cry because it's their only way of communicating,' she said shortly. She felt her tension ratchet up another notch as she tried to feed Harry and he refused to take the teat into his mouth.

'You don't feed him from your breast?' Cortez commented.

'I wasn't able to.' It was another failure that weighed on her conscience but she was in no mood to explain that she had been fighting for her life immediately after Harry's birth. Although she had tried to breastfeed him when she'd come out of Intensive Care, her body hadn't produced enough milk.

'I didn't realise you were an expert in childcare,' she said to Cortez sarcastically. 'It's a pity you weren't around when Harry was born and you could have helped to look after him.'

To her relief Harry finally stopped crying and took his feed. When he finished his bottle she carried him up to the nursery and placed him in his cot. Her headache was worse and she had developed a severe pain in her lower back as well as a high temperature. A phone call to her GP in Sussex confirmed her suspicion that she had all the symptoms of another kidney infection, and she was advised to start the course of antibiotics which she'd been prescribed to treat a recurring infection.

Thankfully, she had brought the antibiotics with her. She swallowed one of the pills and a strong painkiller before she called the nanny's mobile number and explained that she was feeling unwell.

'Do what the doctor said and start the course of antibiotics immediately,' Barbara instructed. 'I'll leave my daughter's right away and I should be in

Kensington by the time Harry wakes up from his afternoon nap.'

Elin was shivering, but when she glanced in the mirror she saw that her face was flushed and her hair was damp with sweat. Hopefully, the high-strength medication would halt the infection before it got too bad, she thought, as she climbed into bed fully dressed and burrowed beneath the duvet in an attempt to get warm. When she'd suffered previous kidney infections the antibiotics had made her feel as unwell as the illness.

She fell into a fitful, feverish sleep. One minute she was hot and the next freezing cold and, as she tossed and turned, her mind was taken over by ter-rifying hallucinations. Distantly she was aware of Harry crying, and she knew she must go to him, but her limbs felt heavy and uncoordinated. She thought she heard a man's deep voice talking to her but she couldn't make sense of what he said. Some time later she felt herself being lifted and carried in a pair of strong arms, but maybe she dreamed it. After that she remembered nothing.

CHAPTER SIX

CORTEZ GAVE UP trying to concentrate on a financial report for Saunderson's Bank after he'd read it three times and still had no idea what it said. Business had been his life since he'd graduated from university with a first class degree and a determination to succeed. His new role as chairman of the prestigious private bank was more proof that he had come a long way from picking grapes at his mother's small vineyard in Jerez. But waiting to learn if he was the father of Elin's child dominated his thoughts and he drummed his fingertips on the coffee table and glanced at his watch for the hundredth time.

When his phone rang and he recognised the number of the paternity test clinic on the screen he took a deep breath before he answered the call. Moments later he ran an unsteady hand across his face.

Santa Madre! He had a son.

Conflicting emotions stormed through him. A fierce joy and pride in his beautiful son, but anger when he thought of the child's mother. Elin had lied about Harry's date of birth and Cortez was furious, knowing that if he had not insisted on a DNA test she might have disappeared with the baby and he would never have known he was a father.

He lurched to his feet. He felt drunk although he had not had a drop of alcohol. He was in shock, he realised. When he'd seen Harry's black hair and dark eyes he had wondered if the baby could be his. But he was unprepared for the overwhelming emotions that poured through him. Driven by a need to see his child, he strode out of the room and quickly climbed the stairs. He heard Harry crying and a feeling he could not begin to describe welled inside him, a fundamental desire to protect his son.

Following the sound of Harry's cries, he located the nursery and was surprised that Elin was not already there to comfort the baby. He stood next to the cot and felt as if his heart was being squeezed in a vice as he stared down at the screaming, red-faced infant. It was incredible that a small baby could make such a loud noise. Yet still Harry's mother did not appear.

Cortez opened a door to an adjoining room and recognised he was in the bedroom where he had spent the night with Elin just over a year ago. Memories assailed him of her wearing a scarlet silk dress and not a lot else besides, he'd soon discovered. Their passion had been electrifying and she had been with him every step of the way. He did not know what to make of her assertion that she'd had sex with him that night because her drink had been spiked with a date-rape drug. The sexual chemistry that had ignited between them when he had kissed her earlier today had been undeniable.

The room was dimly lit by the bedside lamp. He switched on the overhead light and frowned when he saw the top of her blonde head poking above the duvet. 'Elin?' She did not answer, and when Cortez pulled back the covers her eyes flickered open and she stared at him vacantly. Her skin was pale and beaded with sweat. 'Your baby needs you,' he told her. She muttered something incomprehensible and huddled beneath the duvet. Cortez's concern for his son was paramount. 'Does Harry want to be fed?' His jaw tightened. 'For pity's sake, you can't leave him to cry.'

She either did not hear what he said or did not care, and she closed her eyes again. Cortez frowned as he remembered the recent speculation by the media that Elin used recreational drugs. There had been a photo in some of the tabloids of her being carried out of a nightclub in a semi-conscious state. Had she taken an illegal substance this afternoon which had rendered her unable to care for her baby? *His* baby.

He returned to the nursery and hesitated. His heart was pounding and for the only time in his life he felt terrified. He had never held a small baby before, and Harry looked so *breakable*. Taking a deep breath, he reached into the cot and picked Harry up. The baby's cries immediately subsided to little whimpers that tore on Cortez's heart.

'Hey, little man,' he murmured as he held the baby against his shoulder. Harry stared at him with big, dark eyes fringed with long black lashes. He was more beautiful than anything Cortez had ever seen. The baby's Cupid's bow mouth curved into a smile and Cortez felt a constriction in his throat. 'My son,' he said thickly, wonderingly. He was Harry's father and he would *never* abandon his child like his own father had abandoned him. He was instantly smitten with his baby boy, and his heart felt as if it had swelled to twice its size and was filled to overflowing with love for his child. 'I would give my life to protect you,' he whispered to Harry.

He heard a noise and looked round, expecting to see Elin, but it was the nanny standing in the doorway. 'Ah, Miss Lennox.'

'I would have been back from my daughter's earlier, but there was a delay on the Tube,' she explained.

Cortez looked down at the baby he was cradling so carefully in his arms. 'I am Harry's father.'

'Oh, I guessed that,' she said cheerfully. 'He has inherited your colouring rather than his mother's.'

'Elin is asleep and didn't hear the baby crying. She seems…spaced out,' he said tersely.

The nanny nodded and seemed unsurprised. 'She has these episodes quite frequently. Hopefully, she'll be back to herself in a day or two.'

Cortez instinctively held Harry a little tighter. The nanny's words seemed to confirm the suggestion in the tabloids that Elin was a drug user and he resolved to protect his son from his mother, who was obviously unfit to take care of a child. One of the first things he intended to do was arrange for his name to be added to Harry's English birth certificate under the section for father's details. Even more importantly, he wanted to register his son's birth in Spain, which would be Harry's country of residence from now on. But, to do so, he would need Elin's agreement.

He handed Harry over to the nanny so that she could change his nappy. The procedure was one of many things he would have to learn how to do, Cortez mused.

'Miss Lennox...' he smiled at the nanny and turned on the full force of his charm '...may I call you Barbara? You guessed that I am Harry's father and you might also have realised when you saw Elin and I together at Cuckmere Hall that we are reunited.'

The nanny looked embarrassed by his reminder of when she had caught him and Elin kissing. 'I'm very glad for the two of you,' she murmured, 'and for Harry to have both his parents.'

Cortez did not disabuse Barbara of the idea that he and Elin were going to play happy families. 'We have decided to take our son to Spain, and before we left Cuckmere Hall Elin gave me her and Harry's passports.' It was not a lie, more an elaboration of the truth, he assured his conscience.

'Certain reasons make it necessary for me to re-turn to Spain earlier than I'd planned,' he told the nanny. 'In fact, I need to leave tonight to deal with an urgent business matter. As I am sure you will appre-ciate, I am reluctant to leave my son and Elin behind in England, especially when we have just got back together.' He shamelessly pushed the idea that their relationship was the romance of the year.

'I know it is short notice,' he continued, giving Barbara another dazzling smile. 'Would you be pre-pared to accompany us to Spain on my private jet? Elin will be able to rest during the flight, and I'll need you to take charge of Harry because I am a new and inexperienced father.' He thought of a possible problem. 'You will need your passport.'

'As a matter of fact I always carry it with me. Of course I'll be happy to help in any way that I can,' Barbara told him. 'Elin came up to London only last week to shop for clothes to take on a holiday she'd booked to Greece. Would you like me to pack some things for her and Harry, Mr Ramos?'

'Thank you. And Barbara, please call me Cor-tez, as all my friends do,' he murmured. The nanny could be a useful ally in his bid to win custody of his son, he decided. He was a master strategist and he knew the benefits of making a friend in the en-emy's camp.

'Harry.' Elin sat bolt upright and took a shuddering breath when she realised she'd been having a night-

mare. In her dream she had been running down a long corridor and at the end of it was Harry's pram. But when she finally reached the pram and looked inside, it was empty and she had no idea where her son was.

She looked around her bedroom still with a sense of shock. Yesterday, or was it the day before?—she'd lost track of time—her fever had abated and her head no longer felt as if someone was boring into her skull with a pneumatic drill. But her relief had turned to astonishment when she'd found herself in unfamiliar surroundings and Barbara had told her that they were in Cortez's home in Andalucía.

The nanny had explained that Cortez had arranged for them to fly to Spain on his private jet. He had carried Elin into the plane's bedroom and she had been in a deep sleep for the entire journey. A car had collected them from the airport at Jerez and brought them to his mansion, La Casa Jazmín.

'Cortez had to return to Spain urgently, but he did not want to be separated from you and Harry,' Barbara had told Elin. 'I think it is so romantic that the two of you have got back together. Cortez is devoted to his son. He insists on giving Harry his bottle and he has learned how to change nappies.'

Elin had masked her anger because she did not want Barbara to feel guilty that she had been tricked by Cortez into helping him in effect kidnap her and Harry. She hadn't yet seen him to demand an explanation. Barbara said he had visited her room a few times, but on each occasion she had been feverish and she hadn't recognised him.

Worry gnawed in the pit of Elin's stomach as she slid out of bed and went into an adjoining room which Barbara had explained had formerly been a dressing room. Cortez had instructed his staff to transform it into a nursery. Apparently no expense had been spared to equip the nursery and Harry slept in a magnificent hand-carved cot. She walked past the latest addition to the nursery, an enormous wooden rocking horse, and hurried over to the cot.

Her heart missed a beat when she found it empty. For a few seconds she was back in her nightmare, searching desperately for her baby who had disappeared. She spun round at the sound of footsteps and stared frantically at the nanny, who walked into the room carrying a pile of baby clothes. 'Where's Harry?'

'Cortez took him downstairs.' Barbara seemed unaware of Elin's tension. 'He keeps the pram in his study so that he can be near to Harry while he is working.' She looked closely at Elin. 'I told Cortez that you were feeling much better this morning and he asked me to give you a message that he wants you to meet him in his study at eleven o'clock.'

Elin was desperate to immediately go and find her son. She had been ill for a week but it felt like a lifetime since she had held Harry in her arms and smelled his delicious baby scent. But she acknowledged that she could not walk around Cortez's house wearing her nightdress. When she met him in an hour from now she was determined to appear calm and in control, even though her insides were churning as she wondered what, if any, input he intended to have in his son's life now he must have proof from the paternity test clinic that he was Harry's father.

Although she was feeling better, the effort of showering and getting dressed sapped her energy. She was grateful to Barbara for packing some clothes for her before they'd left London. It was unfortunate that the new outfits she'd bought to take to Rhodes for Virginia's wedding were designed to be worn at beach or pool parties, and the short skirts and skimpy tops were more daring than she usually wore.

She chose a pale blue chiffon dress that did at least have sleeves, but when she checked her appearance in the mirror she was dismayed that the floaty skirt was almost see-through. There was no time to change her outfit when a maid came to her room to escort her to Cortez's study, but Elin reminded herself that he would not be interested in how she looked. He'd had sex with her once and had disappeared immediately afterwards. She was just another notch on his bedpost.

As she followed the maid downstairs she could not help but admire the design and décor of the house. The white marble floors and neutral-coloured walls could have made the rooms feel cold, but patterned rugs and brightly coloured cushions and artwork lent interest and a homely feel to the elegant villa. She walked into the study and her eyes were immediately drawn to the large and very regal-looking pram. With a low cry she sped across the room. Her arms were literally aching to hold her baby.

'Harry has just dropped off to sleep and it would be best if you did not disturb him.'

Cortez's peremptory voice made her halt, and she turned her head to see him leaning against his desk. He was wearing a superbly tailored grey suit, a crisp white shirt and dark grey tie and the formality of his clothes made Elin conscious of her insubstantial summer dress. She lifted her eyes up to his face and felt her heart crash against her ribs as she absorbed the perfection of his sculpted features. His lips were curved in a cynical expression but nothing could detract from the sensual impact of his mouth, and she hated herself for the quiver that ran through her.

Anger was her only defence against her awareness of him. 'You had no right to *abduct* me and my son. It's outrageous that you brought us to Spain without my agreement,' she said heatedly.

'You were not in a fit state to agree or disagree to coming here,' he responded coolly. 'And you are forgetting that Harry is my son too.'

Elin cast a yearning look at her baby sleeping peacefully in the pram before she marched over to the desk, determined to show that she was not intimidated by Cortez. 'I have never forgotten that Harry was conceived as a result of the most shameful night of my life.'

Her attention had been riveted on Cortez, but she was suddenly aware that there was someone else in the room and a frisson of unease ran down her spine as she saw an older man with grey hair and a stern face standing by the window.

'This is Señor Fernandez,' Cortez introduced the man. 'He is a lawyer specialising in family law, particularly in cases when there is a dispute between parents over custody of a child.'

Custody! Elin's legs almost gave way but she fought against the dizzy sensation that swept over her, determined she wouldn't faint. 'There is no dispute.' She was pleased she sounded forceful rather than scared. 'I am going to take Harry back home to England as soon as possible. I've already told you that I don't intend to ask you for financial help towards the cost of his upbringing.'

'Harry does not have a home with you in England. If you think I would allow you to take him to live in a partly derelict cottage which, under the terms of Ralph Saunderson's will, is your only asset, think again,' Cortez said in a hard tone.

'You can't keep me a prisoner here.' Panic gripped her as she remembered that he was in possession of her and Harry's passports.

'I prefer the term guest to prisoner,' he drawled. '*You* can leave whenever you wish.' His meaning was sickeningly clear; she could leave, but he would not allow her to take her baby. Elin was tempted to grab Harry and run out of the study with him, but her common sense reminded her that she had no-where to run to.

'Sit down,' Cortez ordered.

Tension coiled in her stomach as she sank down onto the chair he pulled out for her. Cortez waited until the lawyer was also seated, before he took his place behind his desk. 'Señor Fernandez has pre-pared a document for you to read.'

The chill in his voice sent an ice cube slithering down Elin's spine. She picked up the piece of paper Cortez pushed across the desk and as she read down the printed page her heart thudded painfully fast in her chest.

'What the hell is this?' she said thickly when she had finished reading.

His dark brows lifted. 'I believe it is self-explan-atory. I am offering to give you Cuckmere Hall: the house and entire estate, including the vineyards and winery. The current value of the Cuckmere estate is twenty-five million pounds, and I am prepared to offer you an additional ten million pounds which you could invest and use the interest to pay for the running costs of the house and estate. Alternatively, if you de-cide to sell Cuckmere for its market value, you will still receive the additional ten million pounds, which will be transferred directly into your bank account.

'In return,' he continued smoothly, 'you will sign sole custody of Harry over to me with a legally bind-ing guarantee that you will not seek to change or re-verse this decision at any future date.' He ignored her sharply indrawn breath. 'The agreement will take effect immediately when you have signed the document that you have in your hand. My private jet will be available to take you to England, and you will leave here with the deeds of the Cuckmere estate in your possession.'

'This is a joke, right?' Elin moistened her dry lips with the tip of her tongue and saw Cortez's eyes narrow on her mouth. He couldn't be serious, she assured herself. Obviously he had a warped sense of humour. 'You can't really think I would agree to your disgusting offer.'

The lawyer spoke. 'Señor Ramos's offer is extremely generous. I am certain that you would not receive any more from a court judgement.'

Cortez leaned back in his chair and gave her a hard stare. 'Is there something more that you want?'

'Yes, there is.' She was proud that her voice sounded calm while inside she was a seething cauldron of emotions ranging from anger through to a deep sense of hurt that was inexplicable. Why should she care that Cortez believed she would *sell* her son in a deal that would shame the devil? 'I want you to rot in hell.'

Her control was hanging by a thread. Tears stung her eyes but she would not give him the satisfaction of seeing her cry. Carefully she tore the piece of paper she was holding in half and then tore the two halves into quarters and then eighths, her movements jerky with suppressed violence.

'There is nothing you could offer me. All the riches in the world would not tempt me for a nanosecond to give my son away. And especially—*especially*—' her voice rose, sharp with revulsion '—to a man such as you, who treats women like objects, like dirt. If Ralph had not made you his heir you would not have gone to Cuckmere Hall and discovered that you have a son. Harry would have grown up never knowing who his father was.'

She stood up and dragged in a ragged breath. 'You left after you'd had sex with me because I was nothing, just a means of sexual gratification. You treated me like a whore, but what does that make you? How can you be a good and decent father when you did not even bother to find out if I had conceived your child?'

'*Bastante!* Enough.' Cortez jumped to his feet and glared at her across the desk. He turned his head and spoke in Spanish to the lawyer, who immediately got up and hurried out of the room.

'How can you have the audacity to question my suitability to be a father when you are patently unsuitable to be Harry's mother?' Disgust was stamped on Cortez's patrician features. 'If you refuse my offer, which I believe is a fair one, I will seek to be granted custody of my son through legal channels.'

'No court would take a three-month-old baby away from his mother,' Elin said vehemently, but her heart was thumping with fear. Cortez was a rich man and could hire the best lawyers, but she had nothing to her name, apart from a rundown cottage that she could not afford to have repaired.

'A court would not leave a baby with a known drug-user.' He took no notice when she gasped. 'Perhaps you are an addict, or maybe you are in control of your drug habit—for now. But the risk of addiction is high and I do not believe any judge would risk leaving Harry in your care. I certainly will not.'

'I'm not a drug addict.' Elin heard the hysteria in her voice and fought to bring herself under control, aware that Cortez was likely to suggest she was emotionally unbalanced. But she was astounded by his accusation. 'I have never taken any kind of substance, legal or illegal, in my life, apart from the one time that my drink was spiked at my birthday party.'

'I was led to understand from a reliable source that you are a drug-user,' he said coldly. 'Stories of your wild lifestyle have often been reported by the press.'

'*Stories* is right. Half the things the tabloids print are made up.'

He gave her a cynical look. 'Are you saying that photographs of you staggering out of nightclubs on numerous occasions when you were clearly either drunk or high were fake?'

'No, but...'

'If the reports of your affairs with football stars and other minor celebrities weren't true, why did you not demand that the newspapers retracted the stories?'

'I...' Elin trailed to a halt and bit her lip. She couldn't admit that she had deliberately played up for the paparazzi to keep the media's interest away from her brother. Jarek's addiction to vodka, gambling and women—so many women—made *her* supposed wild lifestyle seem tame in comparison. If Cortez learned that Jarek had been going off the rails since Lorna Saunderson's death, he might sack him from Saunderson's Bank.

'Presumably you could not threaten to take legal action against the tabloids because the stories they printed about you were true,' Cortez said grimly. His eyes were chips of obsidian. 'I have been advised by a child psychologist that Harry is too young to have formed a meaningful bond with you, and he will not be adversely affected by a clean break from you when he is only a few months old.'

'Of course he has formed a bond with me,' she choked. 'I am his *mother*. For God's sake, I carried him inside me for nine months, but where were you, his father, then?' Elin's anger turned to despair and she struggled to swallow past the lump that had formed in her throat.

'I was shocked when I realised that my night of shame had resulted in pregnancy,' she admitted. 'And terrified that I had to face my pregnancy alone. All the other women at the childbirth classes had their husbands or partners with them, and I pretended that my baby's father was working abroad because I was too embarrassed to admit I didn't even know his identity.

'I never knew my parents,' she told Cortez huskily. 'They died when I was a baby and my brother was six, and we were placed in an orphanage. I was luckier than other children in the orphanage because at least I had my brother, who took care of me as well as he was able to. My earliest memories are of feeling fear and confusion. I am Bosnian by birth, and the orphanage was in Sarajevo. When the city was bombed during the Bosnian war, many of the orphanage staff were killed or ran away and abandoned the children.'

She was breathing hard, as if she had run a marathon. 'I know what it is like to be abandoned. I will never, ever leave my son. Your vile accusations—especially that I use drugs—are untrue. I love Harry more than life and I would never do anything that might harm him or put him at risk.'

From the pram came a faint cry as Harry stirred. Elin shot across the room. Her heart felt as if it would burst with love as she lifted her baby into her arms and pressed tender kisses to his satin-soft cheek. 'Hello, my angel,' she murmured and was rewarded with a sleepy smile from her little son that filled her with the sweetest joy.

She turned to find that Cortez had followed her over to the pram and he was standing next to her with a tense expression on his face, as if he feared she might drop Harry, she thought furiously. His next words shocked her more than anything else he had said.

'When you discovered you were pregnant, why did you decide to go through with it?'

Elin was counting Harry's eyelashes and only half paying attention to Cortez. 'What do you mean?'

His breath hissed between his teeth. 'Did you consider not having your child?'

She jerked her eyes to his face as his meaning sank into her stunned brain and she felt sick. 'Oh, my God! You think I could have done that? What have I done to deserve your foul accusations? I thought when you suggested I could give away my baby for financial gain that you could not be any more insulting. But I was wrong.'

Something indecipherable glittered in Cortez's eyes. 'It was not an unreasonable question. You said you felt scared when you found out you were pregnant and faced being a single mother.'

Elin shook her head. 'I loved my baby from the minute I knew that a miracle was happening inside me,' she told him fiercely. 'At my ultrasound scan when I was told I was expecting a boy, I felt sad that he wouldn't have a father because I know from my own childhood that a child needs to have security provided ideally by both its parents. A child needs to feel loved. Nothing else is as important.'

She whirled around and walked over to the door with Harry held tightly in her arms. 'I know something else,' she said, turning back to stare at Cortez with disgust in her eyes.

He looked…stunned was the only way she could

describe the expression on his face. His skin appeared to be drawn tight over his razor-sharp cheekbones. The first time she had seen him at her party a year ago he had reminded her of a wolf, and she should have followed her instincts and fled from him while she'd had the chance, she thought grimly.

'I know that your wealth does not mean you will be a good father. You can't *buy* your son. What Harry needs is a father who will always be there for him, but you weren't around when I was in Intensive Care after his birth.' Her voice shook. 'Thankfully my brother spent hours in the hospital nursery with my son. And of course Harry was looked after by the nurses, but he did not have either of his parents with him, just like I didn't have my parents when I lived at the orphanage.'

Cortez frowned 'Why were you in Intensive Care?'

'I bled heavily soon after giving birth.' Elin swallowed hard. It was only three and a half months since Harry had been born and the memories of what had happened in the delivery room—when the euphoria of her son's birth had rapidly turned into a scene from a horror film—were vivid in her mind.

'The medical term is a postpartum haemorrhage. I was terrified I would bleed to death,' she admitted. 'I was rushed into Theatre and given a general anaesthetic, and I don't remember anything after that. But I was told afterwards that I had emergency surgery and a blood transfusion. If the crash team had not been able to stop the bleeding they would have had to perform a hysterectomy, which you probably know is an operation to remove the womb. But luckily the doctors were able to save my life without ending my chances of one day having another child.'

She looked down at her infant son and blinked away her tears that always welled up whenever she thought of how close Harry had been to being motherless and fatherless. 'I'm grateful to my brother for saying he would have adopted my baby if I had died. But at the crucial time when Harry needed his father, you weren't around. So don't preach to me that I am not a suitable mother, because I fought to stay alive for my son and I will fight to the death to keep him.'

CHAPTER SEVEN

FROM THE WINDOW Cortez watched Elin walk across the lawn holding Harry in her arms. She had swept out of the study, leaving him reeling from what she had told him. He went cold at the thought that she could have bled to death following Harry's birth, and guilt knotted in his stomach as he acknowledged the damning truth that if Elin had died he would never have known about his son.

The gazebo next to the swimming pool offered shade from the midday sun, which was strong even in March. Elin sat down on a garden chair and held the baby against her shoulder. Even from a distance Cortez could see the gentle expression on her face as she cradled her son.

A lioness protecting her cub.

The vehement words she'd flung at him a few minutes ago echoed inside his head. *'I fought to stay alive for my son and I will fight to the death to keep him.'* Cortez thought of another woman who had been fiercely protective of her child. His mother had brought him up without any support from his father. Marisol Ramos had been shunned by her family and by many of the villagers, who had judged her for being an unmarried mother. She had worked day in, day out at her small vineyard to earn money to feed and clothe him.

He remembered the recent discovery he had made while he'd been at Cuckmere Hall and had sorted through some of Ralph Saunderson's private papers. He had found an old bank statement which proved that his father *had* given his mother money when she'd told him she was pregnant. But Marisol had not spent the money to make her life easier, and the only explanation Cortez could think of was that she had saved the money to pay for him to go to university.

A good education had given him the means to escape the poverty of his childhood, and it could be argued that he owed his success partly to Ralph's financial contribution. He had been shocked to discover that his father had not completely abandoned him. *Like he had abandoned Elin*. The knot of guilt in his stomach tightened.

But if Elin loved Harry as much as she insisted, why was she a drug-user? She had furiously denied that she was a drug addict and Cortez conceded it was possible that the tabloid stories about her having a drug habit were exaggerated. But in London the nanny had not been unduly surprised when Elin had been incapable of caring for Harry. He had assumed that Elin had been semi-conscious on the flight to Spain as a result of something she had taken, but could there be a different explanation? For his baby son's sake he had to find out the truth about Elin, and his first step would be to talk to the nanny.

Barbara was in the nursery, unpacking the latest delivery of baby clothes and toys that Cortez had ordered for his son. 'Harry will have to be dressed in two new outfits a day if he is going to wear all these lovely clothes before he grows out of them,' she said as she folded a cute sailor suit and placed it in a drawer.

'I'm sorry to give you extra work,' Cortez murmured, glancing at the boxes strewn across the floor. He spied a wooden train set and wondered how old Harry would be before he became interested in toys. He was looking forward to watching his son grow up and he was determined that he would be around when Harry took his first steps and spoke his first words. There had been many times when he was a boy that he'd wished he had a father like the other boys at school. *His* son would never doubt that his father loved him, Cortez vowed.

'To be honest, I like having something to do,' Barbara told him. 'I often feel guilty that I am paid to do very little.'

'Caring for a baby must be a full-time job.'

'Yes, but Elin has always insisted on doing everything for Harry. Even when he went through a period of waking several times in the night, she kept his crib next to her bed so that she could see to him. Of course she couldn't do very much just after she'd given birth and she was weak from losing so much blood. That was why her brother hired me. And then, when Elin was getting her strength back, she developed a serious kidney infection. I do hope that this latest bout of a recurring infection which made her so unwell for the past few days will be the last,' Barbara said. 'The drugs she took to fight the infection are very powerful and, as you noticed, the side-effects absolutely knocked her out.'

Cortez stiffened but he managed to keep his tone casual as he asked, 'What exactly are the drugs Elin took?'

'She was prescribed a powerful penicillin antibiotic to destroy the bacteria that causes the infection. But, as I said, the drug has unpleasant side-effects, which meant that Elin was unable to breastfeed Harry when she developed a kidney infection soon after he was born.'

Cortez stared at the nanny. 'To your knowledge does Elin use recreational drugs, for instance cocaine? There have been reports in some of the more lurid English newspapers that she is involved in the drug culture which is popular in nightclubs,' he persisted when Barbara looked astonished.

'Good heavens, you don't want to believe anything you read in those kinds of papers. They are called the gutter press for a good reason. There was even a story printed last year which stated that Elin was having an affair with a married actor simply because they were photographed leaving a club at the same time. But she'd never even spoken to the man. As for her taking recreational drugs—' the nanny shook her head '—I've never seen any evidence of that, and I simply don't believe it. Elin is the most devoted mother I have ever met and I am absolutely convinced that she would not do anything that could be detrimental to Harry.'

'I see,' Cortez said slowly. The uncomfortable re-alisation was dawning on him that he might have misjudged Elin. And it was not the first time, his conscience reminded him. When he had gone to Cuckmere Hall for the reading of Ralph Saunder-son's will, Elin had told him that he was her baby's father but he had refused to believe her until a DNA test had proved she was telling the truth.

But if she was not a drug-user, and according to the nanny Elin was a good mother, then he was un-likely to win custody of his son in a court battle. And he could not forget that Elin had turned down the chance to own Cuckmere Hall. He knew she loved the house. The value of the estate plus the additional money he'd offered her amounted to thirty-five mil-lion pounds. It was a sizeable fortune and he had believed that she might be tempted, but she had un-hesitatingly rejected his offer and scathingly told him that he could not buy his son.

Even so, could he trust that her apparent devotion to Harry was real? Cortez's jaw hardened. After Al-andra he had vowed never to trust any woman. But Elin was the mother of his child and somehow they were going to have to come to an agreement on how they could both be parents to their son.

Elin had fled from the acrimonious atmosphere in the study and sought refuge in the garden. But when Harry became fretful for his next feed she took him back to the house and her heart sank when she met Cortez in the entrance hall. Revulsion swept through her as in her mind she heard his cold voice offering her Cuckmere Hall if she gave up all rights to her baby. It had been even worse than his accusation that she was a drug addict and she tensed as he strode towards her, fearful of what he was going to say to her, what new insult he might throw at her now. Her wariness must have shown on her face and he frowned when she clutched Harry tightly to her chest.

'*Dios*, you do not need to look so terrified,' he said roughly. 'I am not going to hurt you.'

'Really?' Her voice was brittle, her emotions balanced on a knife-edge. 'You don't think I might have found your disgusting attempt to bribe me to give up my baby hurtful?'

He did not answer but something flashed in his dark eyes that she might have believed was regret if she did not know that Cortez Ramos had a lump of granite where his heart should be.

'I have to go to Madrid on business and I will be away for one night, at the most two,' he said abruptly. 'The trip was planned before I knew about Harry but when I return we will talk about what we are going to do with regard to our son.'

Elin tried to ignore the tug her heart gave when Cortez said *our* son. It gave an impression of unity between them that did not exist, she reminded herself.

'What am I supposed to do while you are able to get on with your life, but I am a prisoner in your house? I demand that you give back my and Harry's passports.'

'If I did give them back would you promise to remain at La Casa Jazmín?' He gave her a sardonic look when she stayed silent. 'If you took Harry away from here I would not rest until I'd tracked you down,' he warned her. 'But to save us both time and effort and spare Harry unnecessary upheaval if you decide to try and disappear with him, I will keep the passports in my possession for now.'

'You have no right…' Elin broke off when she realised that Cortez was not paying her attention and was watching his son avidly. Harry was staring at his father and gave a winsome smile that was guaranteed to melt the stoniest heart. The effect on Cortez was startling. His hard features softened and he murmured something in Spanish as he leaned closer and kissed the top of the baby's head.

Elin's senses stirred as she breathed in the musky scent of Cortez's aftershave. The sight of his dark head against Harry's downy black hair evoked a curious ache in her heart. For a moment she allowed herself to imagine that they were a happy family. In her daydream Cortez kissed his baby son before he moved to cover her mouth with his and kissed her with bone-shaking tenderness and the promise of passion later, when they were alone in each other's arms.

But the reality was that they were at loggerheads and set to fight a custody battle over their son, she reminded herself. It was a battle that she could lose, for Cortez's wealth and power meant he had access to the best lawyers. The idea that she might be ordered by a court to hand over her baby caused icy fingers of fear to wrap around her heart.

She realised that Cortez was looking at her with an odd expression, as if he also wished that the situation between them was different. But that was too much of a stretch for her imagination, she told herself sharply. Cortez had kidnapped her and was keeping her a prisoner. Never mind that La Casa Jazmín was a beautiful house, it was a gilded jail. Cortez had said some vile things to her, and his promise that they would talk when he returned from Madrid had sounded more like a threat. She jerked away from him and whatever it was that had flickered between them disappeared.

He picked up his briefcase and walked across the hall. 'I will be back as soon as I can.'

'Don't rush back on my account,' Elin said coldly. But, absurdly, when he strode out of the house and she heard his car roar off down the drive she immediately missed him. She wondered if he had a mistress in Madrid who he was planning to spend the night with. He was a virile man and he was bound to have a lover. The thought bothered her more than it should have done and she despised herself for feeling jealous as she visualised him having sex with another woman.

In fact Cortez was only away for one night and returned to La Casa Jazmín late the following afternoon. Elin was pushing Harry in his pram around the garden, hoping that the rocking movement would send him off to sleep. Her heart gave an annoying leap when the gates swung smoothly open to allow Cortez to drive through them. He parked his rampantly masculine black sports car in front of the house and leaned against the bonnet, watching her from behind his designer shades as she walked towards him.

The top few buttons on his shirt were undone, revealing a vee of his darkly tanned chest and a sprinkling of black hairs that Elin remembered from a year ago arrowed down over his flat abdomen. She felt heat spread over her face and hoped he would think she was flushed from the warm sun, and not because she was overwhelmingly aware of him.

'I suppose you have a secret code to unlock the gates,' she said as she drew nearer to him. 'Beautiful though the garden is, I am bored of walking around it and I'd hoped to take Harry on a longer walk, perhaps to a village if there is one nearby. But the perimeter gates are locked.' Frustration edged into her voice. 'You have no right to keep me imprisoned.'

Cortez looked unconcerned by her outburst. 'The main gates are activated by car number plate recognition and they are kept locked for security reasons. The village is five miles away but it has no shops and there's little there to excite you.'

'You don't know what excites me,' Elin snapped, irritated by his arrogance.

He threw back his head and laughed, and she was riveted by the sheer beauty of his face, alight with merriment. The rich sound of his amusement reached down to something deep inside her. Laughter made him even more attractive, and he was already too gorgeous for his own good, she thought ruefully.

'Actually, I have vivid memories of what excited you when you lured me into your bed, *querida,*' he murmured.

She pressed her lips together to stop herself from responding to his baiting. She did not want to be reminded of her night of shame a year ago.

'La Casa Jazmín is surrounded by vineyards,' Cortez told her. 'If you like I will show you where you can walk among the vines.'

Despite herself, Elin was curious to see the vineyards that produced the grapes which were used to make the famous Felipe & Cortez brand of award-winning sherry. Cortez led the way across the garden and held open a gate in the wall so that she could push the pram through it.

'I suppose you grow Palomino grapes here,' she said, recognising the dark green leaves on the vines. 'The *albariza* soil type has a high chalk content, perfect for retaining moisture, which is vital during the hot, dry summers you have in this region of Spain. It's interesting that the soil on the South Downs is also chalky, similar to soil in the Champagne region of France. But of course English summers are cooler than here, allowing us to grow Chardonnay and Pinot Noir grape varieties at Cuckmere. At least—' Elin broke off and grimaced '—we grow those grape varieties currently at Saunderson's estate winery, and we have concentrated on producing a sparkling white wine. But you, or whoever buys the estate if you decide to sell it, might decide to grow something else.'

She glanced at Cortez and found him staring at her with evident surprise. 'I did not realise that you took a genuine interest in the winery,' he said.

'It was my adoptive mother's dream to produce an English sparkling wine on a par with Champagne. When Mama died I was determined to continue her work and fulfil her dream, which is why I have a Master's degree in viticulture and oenology. You look shocked,' she said wryly. 'Did you think I was the brainless bimbo that I am portrayed by the tabloids?'

He shrugged. 'You cannot entirely blame the media for your reputation. The paparazzi did not have to look hard to find evidence of your wild life-style. Admittedly, it was months ago that you were regularly seen at the coolest London nightclubs and scandal was never far from you.' He looked at her speculatively. 'What makes me curious is why you seemed to deliberately seek notoriety and the attention of the press.'

Cortez's insight made Elin uneasy. She did not want him to guess that she had sought to keep the paparazzi away from her brother when Jarek's life was in freefall. She looked down the long rows of vines that stretched into the distance. 'How many hectares of vineyards do you have?' she asked in a blatant effort to change the subject.

'Two hundred.' Cortez's voice was drier than the finest Manzanilla sherry and Elin dropped her eyes from his sardonic gaze.

'There are only six hectares of vineyards at Cuckmere. It's lucky you don't have winter frosts this far south,' she told him. 'It would take an army of workers to light frost candles to protect all your vines.'

He helped her to steer the pram around the deep tractor tyre grooves on the path. 'I have heard of the practice of lighting candles to raise the air temperature around the vines to above freezing but I've never seen it done.'

'If you had looked out of the window the night you stayed at Cuckmere Hall you would have seen the vineyards glowing with golden candle lights,' Elin told him. 'There was a frost, but luckily a few of the estate workers stayed up all night to help me light the *bougies*. It would have been a catastrophe if the new shoots on the vines had been frost damaged.'

'So that's why you were still in bed at ten o'clock the next morning,' Cortez murmured in an odd voice. 'I thought you lazed around every morning and left Harry to be cared for by the nanny.'

'Lack of sleep was probably a contributing factor when I developed a kidney infection,' Elin confided. 'Harry had been restless for a few nights before the fund-raising party for Lorna's Gift. When I'm tired my immune system seems to shut down.'

Cortez was still holding the pram handle and Elin caught her breath when his fingers brushed against hers. She looked down at his darkly tanned fingers next to her much paler ones, and memories flooded her mind of his hands roaming over her body, caressing her breasts and slipping between her legs. She was appalled when she felt a molten sensation *there*, where a year ago his skilful touch had given her unbelievable pleasure.

'We should go back to the house before Harry wakes up for a feed,' she said stiltedly, praying that Cortez did not notice her flushed face. She felt hot with shame and a helpless longing that made her angry with herself. How could she want him after the way he had treated her? Where was her self-respect?

'Another time I will give you a tour of the bodega,' Cortez offered. To Elin's relief, he seemed unaware that her hormones were in meltdown. 'Not all the grapes from these vineyards are used to make Felipe & Cortez sherry. About a third of the crop is sold to other wineries.' They had reached the gate in the wall, and he held it open to allow Elin to push the pram through to the garden before he continued speaking. 'Tomorrow evening I am hosting a party for F&C's shareholders and clients. A few media representatives have also been invited. At the party I intend to give a press statement announcing that Harry is my son.'

Elin's heart dropped like a stone. 'Why now? I mean…there is no rush, especially as nothing has been decided yet about who will have custody of him.'

'Whatever happens in the future with regard to arrangements for where Harry will spend his childhood, and with whom, I want to publicly recognise that he is my son.' Cortez frowned when he saw her dismayed expression. 'I'm not going to drop out of his life, however much you might wish that I would,' he said in a hard voice. 'I want to be a full-time parent to him while he is growing up.'

'So do I,' she cried emotionally. 'But you want to take Harry away from me.'

'That's not true. I accept that he needs you, certainly while he is so young. At the party I will introduce you as the mother of my child.'

Her brows rose. 'Aren't you worried I'll turn up in a drug-fuelled haze, out of my head on whatever substance you think I snort up my nose, or inject into my veins?'

To Elin's surprise Cortez looked uncomfortable as he raked a hand through his hair. 'I have realised that I was wrong about you, and you are not in fact a drug-user,' he said gruffly. 'The stories about you in the tabloids seemed to prove that you had a drug habit. But it is now clear to me that you take motherhood seriously.'

'My commitment to Harry has never been in doubt,' she said furiously. 'But you refused to believe he was your son when I first told you.'

His jaw hardened but his response was controlled, as if he was forcing himself to remain calm in the face of her angry condemnation. 'I now have proof that Harry is mine, and tomorrow evening I will make it public knowledge that I am his father. You do not need to worry that I am one hundred per cent committed to my son.'

Cortez smiled at the CEO of a brandy production company which was an important client of Felipe & Cortez Vineyards, and realised that he had no recollection of the conversation he'd had with the other man for the past ten minutes. Over Señor Santana's shoulder he watched Elin chatting to another client, and he gritted his teeth when he noted that the guy looked dazzled by Elin. Cortez understood how that felt.

Desire had jack-knifed through him when he had knocked on her bedroom door fifteen minutes before the guests were due to arrive to escort her downstairs. The day before, he had suggested that he could order an evening gown for her from an exclusive boutique in Jerez, but she had declined his offer, saying she'd brought a dress with her from London that was suitable to wear to the party.

Elin's idea of suitable was not the same as his, Cortez brooded as his eyes followed her obsessively when she moved around the room, stopping frequently to speak to guests. Her long sapphire-blue dress was a deceptively simple silk sheath with a diamanté belt that showed off her tiny waist. The halter-neck style left her shoulders and back bare and her blonde hair was swept up into a chignon, revealing the slender column of her white throat. In truth, the gown was elegant and sensual rather than overtly sexy, but Cortez hated the fact that every man in the room was looking at her and no doubt fantasising about her. He would feel happier if she were wearing a shroud. This possessive feeling was new and unwelcome and he felt irritated that she was the only woman who had such an effect on him.

When she had opened her bedroom door and given him one of those cool smiles of hers that never failed to set his teeth on edge, he had come worryingly close to sweeping her into his arms and carrying her over to the bed. He had wanted to strip her dress from her body and kiss her mouth and her breasts until he heated her up and she turned into the sensual siren who a year ago had begged him in a throaty whisper, that still haunted his dreams, to make love to her.

He forced his mind to the present when his PA came over and told him that everything was ready for him to make a statement to the press. He had asked the nanny to bring Harry downstairs when the baby woke for his ten p.m. feed. Barbara walked into the ballroom and Cortez strode over and took his son from her. As he lifted Harry into his arms, Elin materialised at his side. Her tension was almost tangible.

'Let me hold him,' she muttered. 'He hasn't long been fed, and he might be sick on your tuxedo.'

'I don't give a damn about my jacket.' He stared at his son and Harry stared right back with his big, dark eyes flecked with gold. The baby's rosebud mouth curved into a smile of recognition and Cortez silently repeated his vow that he would willingly sacrifice his life to protect his little boy.

The room fell silent as he made his way to one end of the ballroom, where a group of journalists were assembled in front of a microphone. There was a ripple of interest from the audience as he stepped onto the podium holding the baby in his arms. He held out his hand to Elin and she hesitated before she walked up to stand beside him.

He had given prior instruction that the press conference would be conducted in English for Elin's benefit. 'Ladies and gentlemen, the continued success of Felipe & Cortez, which is reflected in the latest rise in profits, makes me very proud. But I am even prouder to introduce my son, Harry Ramos.'

The news was met with murmurs of surprise and

interest from the guests. Cortez's PR team had arranged that the press could ask a few pre-arranged questions, but as the session drew to an end a journalist stood up and asked an unplanned question.

'Do you have any plans to marry your son's mother? And, if so, when will the wedding be?'

Cortez smiled to hide his irritation with the journalist. 'Miss Saunderson and I are not prepared to make a statement with regard to our personal situation yet,' he said smoothly.

'Miss Saunderson is English, and I am sure that your shareholders would like to know if you will continue to live in Spain, Señor Ramos, or if you plan to move to England to be with your son and his mother.'

'Felipe & Cortez's shareholders can be assured that I will continue to be based in Spain and my commitment to the company and also to my role as CEO of Hernandez Bank is unchanged.'

'Will your son also live in Spain?'

'Of course. Harry is my heir and when he is older I hope he will develop the same passion that I have to grow the best grapes and produce the best sherry for which F&C is renowned.'

'But you do not intend to get married and your son will remain illegitimate?' the journalist persisted.

'As I have already stated, I do not intend to make any further announcement about my private life right now,' Cortez said tersely. 'All I will say is that the current situation regarding my son's legitimacy will be resolved in the very near future.'

He signalled to his PA that the press conference was over and stepped down from the podium. As he carried Harry out of the ballroom Elin hurried after him, and he guessed from the staccato beat of her stiletto heels on the marble floor that her temper was simmering.

'What did you mean by that last vague reply you gave to the journalist?' she demanded after Cortez handed Harry to the nanny so that she could take him back upstairs to the nursery. The entrance hall was full of guests who were preparing to leave now that the party was over, and he led Elin into his study and locked the door to ensure their privacy. She put her hands on her hips. 'How can Harry's legitimacy be resolved?'

He waited a heartbeat. 'By us getting married.'

'Very funny,' she snapped. 'But I'm not in the mood for jokes.'

'It wasn't a joke. I'm serious.' In his mind Cortez heard the journalist say that Harry was illegitimate, and he was hurtled back in time to when he had been taunted by other boys in the village where he had lived with his mother. *'Malparido!'* they had shouted at him. The word meant bastard in English. Worse had been when they had called his mother a *puta*—a whore. Cortez had retaliated to the boys' insults with his fists. He hadn't cared what they called him, but he had fought to defend his mother's honour. Working in the vineyard from an early age had made him physically strong, and after a while the boys had stopped calling him names to his face because they knew he would retaliate with punches.

Attitudes had changed in the thirty-four years since he had grown up among villagers who had held traditional values and sneered at him because his mother was unmarried. But the journalist's comments showed that there was still a stigma attached to being illegitimate. He would not allow his son to be called a *malparido*.

He looked at Elin's mutinous expression and knew he would have a battle on his hands to persuade her to marry him. But she wanted Harry as much as he did and Cortez was prepared to play dirty to get *everything* he desired.

CHAPTER EIGHT

'WHAT MAKES YOU think I'd marry you after you have kidnapped me, insulted me and accused me among other things of being a drug addict?'

Elin's chest heaved as she struggled to control her overwrought emotions. When Cortez had announced to his party guests and the press that Harry was his son, she had felt a sense of being trapped and powerless. 'This ridiculous situation has gone on long enough,' she said forcefully. 'I don't know why you told the journalist that Harry will live in Spain. His home is in England with me.'

Instead of replying, Cortez picked up a crystal decanter and poured a generous measure of pale gold liquid into a glass. 'Do you want a drink?' he asked her. 'This is F&C's finest fifteen-year-old cask-aged sherry.' When Elin shook her head he lifted the glass to his lips and swallowed half its contents in one gulp, almost as if he had needed the hit of alcohol. He looked at her with an unfathomable expression in his eyes. 'So how do you think it will work if we share custody of Harry?'

'What do you mean?'

'Will we each have him living with us for a week or a month at a time? That might work while he is a baby, but when he's older don't you think he will find it unsettling to be shipped between England and Spain like he is a parcel? Is that what you want for our son?'

'Of course not.' A memory flashed into Elin's mind of herself as a little girl, walking up the front steps of Cuckmere Hall for the first time after Ralph and Lorna Saunderson had adopted her and taken her to England. She had only known the orphanage in war-torn Sarajevo, but even though it had not been a happy place she had been scared to leave. Moving away from familiar surroundings was unnerving for a child. She remembered how she had clung to her brother's hand for reassurance. How would Harry feel when he was a bit older and he was separated from one of his parents and taken to live with his other parent in a different country every few weeks? Not having a permanent home would be unsettling for him.

'What about Christmases and birthdays?' Cortez went on relentlessly. 'How much do you think he will enjoy those special occasions if he has to choose which of his parents to spend them with?'

'Plenty of parents manage to lead separate lives and successfully share custody of their children,' Elin argued. 'We don't have to get married for Harry's sake.'

'No, we don't *have* to,' Cortez agreed flatly. 'But why *wouldn't* we choose to give our son stability, security and the consistency of growing up with both his parents? Harry needs to be part of a family and surely his needs are paramount?'

'This is crazy!' Elin's frustration bubbled over. Everything Cortez had said made sense, but marry him…*really*? 'You are the last man on earth I'd choose to marry.'

'Yet, if I am to believe what you told me, I am the first and possibly only man you've had sex with,' he drawled.

She flushed. 'I explained why I slept with you on my birthday night. I certainly wasn't tempted to sleep with anyone else after I'd found out that I was pregnant by a stranger who had gatecrashed my party.'

Cortez finished his drink and set his glass down on the desk. 'I hired a private investigator in England, who checked police records and confirmed that a male guest at your birthday party was accused of tampering with several of the women's drinks. Tom Wilson was charged with administering a substance which is a well-known date-rape drug.'

Elin gave a deep sigh. 'There is the proof that I behaved out of character when I went to bed with you. The drug that had been slipped into my drink without my knowledge had the effect of lowering my inhibitions.' Deep down, she knew she could not only blame the date-rape drug for the way she had responded to Cortez's smouldering sensuality. She had taken one look at him and been blown away by his handsome looks, but she wasn't about to admit that to him.

She became aware that he had moved closer to her without her noticing him doing so. He possessed the stealth and predatory instincts of a wolf stalking its prey. The thought unnerved her even as her body reacted to the evocative scent of his cologne. He was always impossibly handsome, but tonight, wearing an impeccably tailored black dinner suit, he took her breath away. It hurt her to look at him and she wanted to turn her head away, but he trapped her gaze and the sultry heat in his gold-flecked eyes sent a sizzle of electricity through her.

'You can tell yourself that it was a drugged drink that made you desire me a year ago, but it doesn't explain your response when I kissed you at Cuckmere Hall,' he drawled.

'You took me by surprise.' She was quick to defend her actions but she flushed guiltily as she remembered how she had melted in his arms. She held up her hand to ward Cortez off when he stepped even closer to her. He was so tall that she had to tilt her head to look at his face and the implacable expression stamped on his chiselled features caused her heart to miss a beat.

'What are you doing? Leave me alone.' Her panicky plea was muffled against his mouth as his head swooped down and he crushed her lips beneath his in a kiss designed to prove that he was her master.

She must not succumb to his sensual magic, Elin told herself frantically. But she felt boneless as Cortez pulled her into the heat and strength of his big body, making her aware of his powerful abdominal muscles and, lower down, the shockingly hard ridge of his arousal that pressed insistently against her pelvis.

He deepened the kiss, exploring the moist interior of her mouth with his tongue while he slid one hand into her hair and clamped her skull so that escape was impossible. His other hand skimmed down her bare back, his touch setting her skin alight before he spread his fingers over the swell of her buttocks. Her silk dress was a frustrating barrier and Elin longed to feel his hands on her naked bottom. Heat coursed through her veins, evoking a carnal craving that mocked her belief that she was not a sensual person.

He continued his exploration of her feminine curves and stroked his way up her body to her breasts. She caught her breath when he pushed the top of her dress aside and played with one nipple, rolling the hard peak between his fingers. Pleasure arced down to the sweet spot between her legs and multiplied a thousand times when he unfastened the halter straps on her dress and bared her breasts to the mercy of his mouth. She felt his warm breath on her skin before he took her nipple into his mouth and sucked hard until she whimpered with pleasure and he transferred his lips to her other breast.

The last vestiges of Elin's resistance crumbled and she gave a low moan of surrender as she wound her arms around his neck. He lifted his head to plunder her mouth with his wicked tongue. In a distant recess of her mind she acknowledged that Cortez had given a masterclass in domination which had rendered her helpless against the onslaught of his passion. A warning voice in her head whispered that she would pay a heavy price in humiliation for these moments of pleasure.

She was right. He suddenly released her and she swayed on her feet, feeling utterly bereft. She lifted her fingers to her mouth and touched its swollen contours. God knew what she looked like. She could feel that her hair had half fallen out of its chignon, and her hands shook as she pulled the top of her dress up over her breasts to hide her swollen, reddened nipples that were still damp from Cortez's tongue. She might as well have shouted from the rooftop that she was his for the taking, she thought in self-disgust.

'Our marriage will provide our son with the security of growing up with both his parents, which is something we know from our childhood experiences is important.' Cortez's voice was coolly unemotional and Elin's stomach gave a sickening lurch as she realised that he was unaffected by what had just happened. Why didn't she learn? A year ago he had left her after they'd had sex, and he had only kissed her now to prove that she couldn't resist him.

'You can't possibly want me for your wife,' she said desperately.

'I have just demonstrated what I want.' He dropped his gaze to the betraying hard peaks of her breasts and smiled cynically. 'What we both want. And there will be other compensations to our marriage of expediency in addition to our sexual compatibility.'

He made it sound so clinical, Elin thought bleakly. 'Your knowledge of viticulture and your ability to walk into a room and instantly charm every person present will be useful when you act as my hostess at social and business functions. My shareholders will love you,' Cortez said drily.

'I don't actually care what your shareholders think of me. What concerns me is how could we possibly create a happy home and family life for Harry when there is so much antipathy between us?' She bit her lip. 'We hardly know each other.'

'Then we had better go on a crash course to learn about each other, hadn't we, *querida*?' His softer tone was unexpected and made Elin wish that the situation was different. If only Cortez loved her.

Shock jolted through her and she told herself not to be stupid. It was bad enough that he made her body feel out of control, and she was not going to lose control of her heart too. She stiffened when he lifted his hand and traced his thumb across her kiss-stung lips.

'Our son was conceived by mistake,' he said quietly, 'but although we may not know each other very well yet, I am confident we agree on one thing. Neither of us regrets for one second that we have been blessed with Harry. For his sake, let us endeavour not to make any more mistakes.'

Perhaps her doubts showed in her expression because he stepped away from her and said coolly, 'Don't forget that by marrying me you'll fulfil the terms of Ralph's will, which stipulates that you can only inherit fifty per cent of Saunderson's Wines if you marry within a year. I have decided not to sell the Cuckmere estate because, as you pointed out, it is Harry's heritage. If you marry me you will be able to continue the work your adoptive mother started when she planted the vineyards, and hopefully produce a top quality English sparkling wine.'

Owning a share of the winery would give her financial security and independence, Elin brooded. Cortez had played his trump card. He knew how much Saunderson's Wines meant to her, and her desire to fulfil Mama's dream. It made sense to agree to marry him to secure her position as Harry's mother and also to take part-ownership of the winery that she had invested so much of her time and energy in.

'All right,' she said abruptly, before she could change her mind. 'I'll marry you for the reasons you have mentioned. I agree that it will be better for our son if we bring him up together. And I am determined to make Saunderson's Wines a successful business.'

Cortez nodded and poured himself another drink, which he swallowed in one gulp. 'I'll make the necessary arrangements for us to marry as soon as possible,' he told her in a crisp tone which indicated that he regarded their marriage as purely a matter of convenience, which of course it was for her too, Elin assured herself.

The bureaucratic process of applying to marry in Spain was fairly long-winded, and it was three weeks later before Cortez was able to book the wedding ceremony at the local Town Hall.

Although he was impatient at the delay in becoming his son's legal parent, he had nevertheless found it fascinating to watch Harry develop. It was astonishing how much the baby had grown and changed in a few short weeks, he said to Elin at Harry's bathtime one evening. The hours they spent together with their son had given Cortez an opportunity to prove his desire to be a good father and he had noticed a gradual thaw in Elin's attitude towards him. He knew he had hurt her with his accusations, and it would take time to win her trust, but he was determined to do so, and show her that they could have a successful marriage.

Now it was the day before their wedding and they were on their way to Seville to have lunch with his married friends, Nicolás and Teresa García. The couple had a one-year-old son, and Cortez hoped that Elin would enjoy spending time with other parents after she'd complained that she felt cut off from her friends in Sussex while she was living in Spain.

He briefly took his eyes from the road and glanced at her sitting beside him in the front of the car. 'What kind of man was Ralph Saunderson?' he asked her. 'It feels strange that I know nothing about my father.' He thought of the man he had met once a year ago. He had not seen Ralph Saunderson after that first visit to Cuckmere Hall and Ralph had not been in contact again before his death. 'You were his adopted daughter and you must have known him well.'

Cortez focused back on the highway, which was bordered on both sides by acres of vineyards stretching to the horizon, and tried unsuccessfully to ignore his fierce awareness of Elin. The light floral perfume she wore stirred his senses, and the expanse of slender thigh exposed by her skirt, that had ridden up when she'd climbed into the car, made him wish that he could pull over by the side of the road and make love to her. But relieving his sexual frustration was not possible for many reasons, not least because Harry was asleep in his baby seat in the back of the car.

Their wedding could not come soon enough, he brooded. Sometimes he had caught Elin looking at him in a way that made him wonder if she was as desperate as he was for them to share a bed. He certainly hoped she was. But he'd heard genuine concern in her voice when she had said that they hardly knew one another, and for that reason he had forced himself to suppress his desire while he concentrated on making her feel at ease with him. He'd never taken as many cold showers as he had recently, he thought wryly.

Elin shifted in her seat and the pretty, floral-patterned dress she was wearing rode a little further up her thighs. She had lost the gaunt look she'd had when Cortez had brought her to Spain, and her unhealthy pallor had been replaced with a light golden tan. Her long hair was tied in a braid that fell over one shoulder and she looked utterly lovely and wholesome and at the same time incredibly sexy. His fingers itched to undo the buttons running down the front of her dress and discover if she was wearing a bra.

'I didn't really know Ralph very well,' she said. 'I wasn't close to him like I was to my adoptive mother. He had a tendency to start many projects with plenty of enthusiasm but he became bored quickly. I think he only agreed to adopt me and my brother because Mama wanted us. She couldn't have children of her own, and when she saw news coverage of the devastation in Sarajevo she was keen to give a home to orphaned children.' Elin grimaced. 'Jarek said that we were another of Ralph's projects and he soon lost interest in us.'

She turned her head to look over her shoulder and check on Harry and Cortez breathed in the lemony scent of her hair. 'On the surface we appeared to be the perfect family, but the truth was that Ralph had affairs with other women,' Elin said flatly. 'I'm sure

Mama chose to ignore his infidelities because she did not want Jarek and me to suffer more upheaval if she and Ralph divorced.'

Elin fell silent when they reached the centre of Seville and Cortez needed to concentrate on driving in heavy traffic. Finally he turned the car onto a driveway in front of the Garcías' elegant villa.

'Don't be nervous,' he said softly when he saw her tense expression. 'This is an informal occasion, and Teresa and Nic are charming people.' He climbed out of the car and carried Harry in his baby seat up the front steps of the house. A maid opened the door and Cortez slipped his arm around Elin's waist as they stepped out of the bright sunshine into the cool hallway. 'Our wedding is tomorrow, and we need to put on a convincing act in front of people that we are a happily engaged couple,' he murmured when she stiffened.

'Why does it matter what other people think about our relationship?' she muttered.

'I don't want rumours to spread that we are marrying for practicality so that we can both bring up our son. Harry is only a baby now, but when he is older he might be teased by other kids at school. How do you think he would feel if he learned that his parents had only married for his sake?' Memories of when he had been taunted by the other boys at school because he did not have a father made Cortez determined that his son would never have reason to feel embarrassed about his parentage.

The maid showed them into a large salon with glass doors that opened onto an attractive courtyard garden. A man and woman came towards them, smiling warmly, and Cortez introduced Elin to Teresa and Nicolás before proudly showing off his son. Harry looked adorable in his blue and white striped outfit and seemed quite happy to be the centre of attention when the other guests crowded around to make a fuss of him. Elin visibly relaxed after a few minutes as she chatted to Teresa and admired the Garcías' son Luiz, who had recently learned to walk.

'Hola, cariño,' a woman's seductive voice murmured close to Cortez.

'Sancha.' He greeted his ex-mistress with a cool smile and tried to suppress his irritation when she linked her arm possessively through his. 'I did not realise you would be here today.'

'I wouldn't have missed my sister's party for the world when Teresa told me that *you* would be coming,' she assured him softly. She leaned forwards so that her breasts were in danger of spilling out of her low-cut dress. 'I was surprised you did not mention that you had accepted an invitation to the party when we met in Madrid a few weeks ago.'

Fortunately, Nic came over to ask Cortez what he and Elin would like to drink, and Sancha sashayed across the room back to her latest lover, who, Cortez happened to know, was some twenty years older than her and a multimillionaire. He almost felt sorry for the guy.

Would Sancha have turned down a mansion and estate worth thirty-five million pounds? It was unlikely, he thought cynically. He turned his head towards Elin and watched her carefully lift Harry out of the baby carrier. Her face was soft with love for her baby. She glanced over and returned Cortez's smile and he felt his heart kick in his chest.

In twenty-four hours she would be his wife and he was surprised by how relaxed he felt at the prospect. He had not planned to marry, certainly not at this stage of his life. But discovering that he had a child had changed everything. He would not allow his son to be illegitimate. Elin had shown herself to be a devoted mother, and perhaps it was time that he let go of the past, and Alandra's terrible betrayal, and learned to trust his soon-to-be wife.

The Garcías' party was the first occasion that Elin had taken Harry out in public. She had hidden away at Cuckmere Hall after his birth, partly because she had needed to recover her strength following the postpartum haemorrhage, but mainly because she could not bear the idea of the tabloids branding her an irresponsible single mother and all the speculation there was bound to be about the identity of her baby's father.

Cortez looked shocked when she admitted that she had kept Harry's birth a secret. 'Are you ashamed of our son?'

'Of course not.' She looked over to where Teresa was holding Harry while she and Cortez helped themselves to lunch from the buffet table. 'I am ashamed of myself,' she said in a low tone, 'and my behaviour when I met you at my birthday party. You probably don't believe me, but I had never slept with any man before that night.'

Cortez speared a king prawn viciously with a fork and transferred it to his plate. 'I wish I had realised you were a virgin,' he said in a taut voice that Elin had never heard him use before. She could almost believe he cared about her feelings until she reminded herself that he was being attentive to her at the party because they were pretending to be in love. She should not read anything into the way he smiled whenever their eyes met, as if she were the only woman in the room.

She glanced down at the sparkling engagement ring on her finger, a square-cut sapphire surrounded by white diamonds. It was the most exquisite ring Elin had ever seen and she could only guess how much it was worth. When Cortez had slipped it onto her finger a few days after she'd agreed to marry him she had protested that she could not accept a valuable piece of jewellery from him. He'd replied that the engagement ring would prove to people that their relationship was genuine, but then he had made her heart leap when he'd said he had chosen the sapphire because it matched the colour of her eyes.

The party was a relaxed affair and Elin found she was enjoying the good food and wine and the chance to socialise with Cortez's friends. A few other couples had young children, and she began to think that living at La Casa Jazmín would not be as isolating as she'd feared. Although she would have to learn to speak Spanish quickly, Elin decided. The other guests all spoke to her in English but they slipped back into speaking Spanish among themselves. She and Cortez had already agreed that Harry would be brought up to be bilingual but she was worried that if she did not master Spanish she would feel alienated from her son and husband.

Husband! Her heart lurched when she thought of her wedding tomorrow. Since she had woken up at La Casa Jazmín nearly a month ago and discovered that Cortez had brought her to Spain while she'd been ill with a kidney infection, her life had seemed unreal. And her sense of unreality had increased over the past weeks as Cortez's attitude towards her had changed radically.

He was no longer cold and stern, and it was hard to believe he had made those horrible accusations that she was a drug-user and an unfit mother. It was as if he was now determined to charm her, and he did not have to try very hard, she acknowledged ruefully as she looked across the room to where he was standing by the glass doors that opened onto the garden. Late afternoon sunshine filled the courtyard garden and danced over his hair so that it gleamed as black as a raven's wing. His black jeans moulded his powerful thighs, and his cream shirt was open at the throat, showing his tanned skin and a sprinkling of black hairs that Elin knew, from when she had watched him swimming in the pool at home, grew thickly over his chest.

She realised with a jolt that she had mentally thought of La Casa Jazmín as home. Tomorrow night would she and Cortez consummate their marriage in the master bedroom? Anticipation coiled in the pit of her stomach. They had not discussed the terms of their marriage, but the hungry gleam in his gold-flecked eyes told her that he desired her, and she had decided that she wasn't going to hide behind her pride and deny that she craved physical intimacy with him. He was her only lover. But he was more than that, for his charm offensive these past weeks had captured her heart and deep down she knew she was falling in love with him.

Harry behaved beautifully for the entire afternoon, but by early evening he became fractious and Elin took him into a small sitting room away from everyone so that she could feed him in peace. She changed his nappy and had just placed him in his baby carrier, ready for Cortez to put him in the car for the drive home, when the door opened and a woman walked into the sitting room.

Elin had met Teresa's sister Sancha earlier in the day. She smiled, trying to ignore a little flicker of feminine jealousy of the Spanish woman's stunning looks. It was no surprise that Sancha worked as a presenter for a national television station in Madrid, she mused. Sancha's gorgeous figure looked as if it had been poured into her tight-fitting white dress, and the colour was a perfect foil for her smooth olive-gold skin. Her jet black hair had been cut into an asymmetric bob that showed off her high cheekbones and flashing dark eyes.

Sancha closed the door and strolled over to sit down on a chair opposite Elin. 'I'm glad to have a few moments alone with you,' she murmured. 'I must congratulate you.'

Despite the other woman's apparently friendly tone, Elin was aware of undercurrents swirling in the room. She looked at Harry, who had fallen asleep in the baby carrier. 'Thank you. I feel very lucky to have a beautiful son and so does Cortez.'

'Mmm…' Sancha did not glance at the baby. 'It was clever of you to turn up and present Cortez with his son. I suppose you had guessed that, having suffered the stigma of being born to an unmarried mother himself, he would not allow his child to be illegitimate. That is the reason he is marrying you, isn't it?'

'I really think that is between me and Cortez,' Elin said politely, but her insides were knotted with tension as she waited for Sancha to get to the point. She did not have to wait long.

'It's all right; he explained it all to me.' The Spanish woman gave a little feigned laugh when she saw Elin's expression. 'Oh, didn't you know that Cortez and I were lovers?'

She hadn't known for sure, but Elin had suspected.

Several times during the afternoon she had noticed Sancha and Cortez standing apart from the other guests, their dark heads bent close as they spoke intently. There had been an incident when Sancha had asked Cortez to get her a drink and he hadn't had to ask what she wanted; he'd simply brought her a glass of white wine. The seemingly insignificant event had revealed an intimacy to their relationship that went far beyond that of casual acquaintances. But Elin was not going to let Sancha know that she felt as if she had been stabbed through her heart.

'Cortez is a very attractive man, and I'd be surprised if he hadn't had other lovers in his past.'

Sancha gave her a speculative look. 'It's good that you have a sensible attitude to his relationship with me. He often has business in Madrid and he always stays at the apartment he bought for us. Would you like to see a picture of it?' She took her mobile phone from her purse and held it out. Elin didn't want to look at the photo on the screen but her eyes were drawn to the image of a bare-chested Cortez lying on a bed with a sheet draped over his hips.

'The apartment only has one bedroom, but it has a very big bed,' Sancha said coyly, twisting the knife into Elin's heart. 'I took this photo the last time Cortez was in Madrid three weeks ago.'

Elin almost choked on the bile that rose in her throat. Three weeks ago, Cortez had told her he was going to Madrid for business, and he'd stayed away for the night. When he had returned to La Casa

Jazmín he had suggested that they get married so that they could both be full-time parents to Harry. But he must have told Sancha of his intention to marry the mother of his child. How else would the Spanish woman have known that it was a marriage of convenience? Elin thought grimly.

She stood up and busied herself with packing Harry's bottle, bib and other paraphernalia into the changing bag while she stifled the hurt that ripped through her. Pride came to her aid and she gave Sancha a bland smile.

'I can guarantee that in future if Cortez has business in Madrid he will come home the same day because he won't want to be apart from his wife and son for even one night.' She held out her hand to Sancha and took a small triumph from the Spanish woman's look of surprise. 'It was nice to meet you,' she murmured before she picked up Harry in the baby carrier and forced herself to walk unhurriedly out of the room.

But Sancha's poison drip-fed into Elin's mind on the journey back to La Casa Jazmín. Cortez seemed convinced by her explanation that she was tired after he'd remarked that she was very quiet. She closed her eyes to shut out his handsome profile while her thoughts went round and round in her head.

She accepted that he must have had countless affairs with beautiful women in his past. Elin could even accept that Sancha had been his mistress. But three weeks ago he had vowed to fight for custody of

his son and he had even offered her Cuckmere Hall
if she signed custody of Harry over to him. Despite
being desperately hurt by his accusation that she
was a drug addict, in a strange way she had felt reassured by Cortez's determination to take care of his
son. But now she knew that on the same day he had
vowed to fight to keep Harry he had visited Sancha
in Madrid and spent the night with her. So much for
Cortez's promise that he would be a devoted father.
He hadn't given Harry a thought when he'd rushed
off to have sex with his lover, Elin thought bitterly.

She recalled their conversation when they had
been driving to the Garcías' house and Cortez had
asked her what kind of man his father had been.
Ralph Saunderson had had a low boredom thresh-
old, which presumably was the reason why he'd had
numerous extra-marital affairs and why he had lost
interest in his adopted children. Elin remembered
how, as a child, she had studied hard at school, hoping to impress her adoptive father, but his disinter-
est had decimated her self-confidence and left her
feeling worthless.

What if Cortez grew bored of fatherhood? She
couldn't bear to think of Harry when he was older,
trying to please his father and make him proud, but
then feeling a failure if Cortez rejected him. Cortez
had never had a chance to know Ralph but it was
likely that he had inherited some of his father's traits.
And perhaps, like his father, he did not consider fi-
delity important in marriage. Elin had a sudden flash

of insight to a future where she was tormented by jealousy and suspicion every time they attended a social event and she wondered which beautiful woman was her husband's latest mistress.

She couldn't do it. She couldn't go through with the wedding when she knew that Cortez was only marrying her out of duty. He had stated that marriage was the best option to give Harry a settled upbringing. But how could a childhood marred by his parents' rows and recriminations be good for Harry?

Cortez's phone rang as they walked into La Casa Jazmín. He frowned when he checked the name of the caller. 'I need to speak to the head of the Japanese branch of Saunderson's Bank,' he told Elin. 'Can you manage Harry on your own?'

'Of course I can.' Was he implying that he didn't think she had been capable of looking after her baby before he'd arrived on the scene like some knight on a white charger to take up his role as Harry's father? she thought irritably. She had managed perfectly well for the past couple of days while the nanny had taken annual leave to do some sightseeing in nearby Cadiz.

She took Harry up to the nursery. He was fast asleep and looked so comfortable in the baby carrier that she decided not to risk waking him by moving him into his cot. But there was another reason to leave him in the baby seat. A crazy plan was forming in her mind, which, the more she thought about it, seemed to be her only option. She did not want to marry Cortez tomorrow. Too much was at stake, not least her heart. But if she refused he had threatened to fight her in court for custody of Harry.

In her bedroom she opened the bedside drawer and took out her and Harry's passports, which Cortez had returned to her a week ago. She had regarded the gesture as a sign that he trusted her not to take their son away. But perhaps he believed that she had fallen under his spell and was too besotted with him to consider leaving, she thought grimly.

She knotted her fingers together, wishing she knew what to do. As far back as she could remember she had been able to ask her brother for advice, but when she had phoned him in Japan to tell him that Cortez was Harry's father and she was going to marry him, Jarek had sounded terse and distracted and had said she should do whatever was best for her and her baby.

Would a loveless marriage to Cortez be best for her and for their son? An image flashed into Elin's mind of stunning Sancha, and she wondered how she could have believed that Cortez desired *her* when he had an exotic mistress in Madrid, and quite possibly several other mistresses dotted around Europe. She had spent her childhood trying, and failing, to please her adoptive father and she was not going to spend her adult life feeling a failure as Cortez's convenient wife.

CHAPTER NINE

ELIN'S ESCAPE PLAN had seemed easy in theory. But in practice she struggled to strap Harry's baby seat into the car when her hands were shaking. She consoled herself with the thought that she would not have to drive Cortez's powerful sports car that roared like a savage beast and would no doubt have woken the entire household. Recently he had bought a family estate car for her to use, but she'd never driven on the right-hand side of the road and she had been glad when he'd sat beside her to give her confidence on her first outing to a nearby village. Now she was planning to drive some twenty kilometres to the airport in Jerez de la Frontera in the dark, and her stomach was knotted with nervous tension.

She waited until midnight before she took Harry in the baby carrier downstairs and collected the car keys from the utility room. The car's engine purred quietly as she drove out of the garage. The main gates at the bottom of the driveway were activated by number plate recognition and should have swung open as the car approached them, but Elin's heart sank when they remained shut.

'Open, damn you,' she muttered. She had spent hours of soul-searching before she'd made the decision to leave Cortez and take Harry back to England, and now that she had got this far with her plan she did not want any delay. She was not going to deny Cortez a role in Harry's life, but it could not only be on his terms.

She switched off the engine and checked that Harry was still asleep before she got out of the car and walked up to the gates with little hope that she would be able to open them manually. To her surprise, when she leaned against one of the gates, it moved. She pushed both gates fully open and stood on the road outside the grounds of the house. Above her the moon was a silver disc in the black sky. She stared up at the stars that glittered as brilliantly as the diamonds on her engagement ring that she had left in Cortez's study with a note explaining her reasons for leaving.

There was nothing to stop her getting into the car and driving away from La Casa Jazmín—except for her conscience. She tried to imagine how Cortez would feel when he discovered that she had taken his son. He would be devastated because he loved Harry. The truth struck her like a lightning bolt. From the moment Cortez had received proof that Harry was his, he had constantly shown that he adored his baby son. With brutal honesty, Elin acknowledged that she'd felt a little bit jealous of the attention Cortez paid to Harry and his love for his son that was so obvious.

Behind her she heard a faint click and she spun round to find that the gates had smoothly and silently closed and she was locked outside Casa Jazmín's grounds, while the car with Harry inside was on the other side of the gates. Frantically, she tugged the gates but they would not budge. Her heart thudded painfully in her chest. The moon had disappeared behind a cloud and the darkness seemed menacing as the horror of her situation sank in.

She could not understand how the electronic gates had started working again. But when the moon reappeared and cast a ghostly gleam along the driveway, the answer stood before her in the form of a six foot four, furiously angry man.

'*Cortez.*' Elin swallowed as she waited for him to speak. The moonlight slanted over his harsh features and his anger was evident in the rigid set of his jaw. But he said nothing as he lifted the baby seat out of the car and walked back towards the house with Harry.

She rattled the metal gates, fear cramping in her stomach. '*Cortez*, please let me in.' He carried on walking as if she hadn't spoken, as if she did not exist. '*Please...*' A sob tore through her. 'You can't take my baby.'

'You were going to take him away from me.' Finally he halted and turned around. His voice was as dark and menacing as the night. 'By chance I went into my study to look for some paperwork, and when I found your note I deactivated the electronic gates. But if I hadn't been in time you would have driven off with Harry. *Dios*, I trusted you, Elin. Something I vowed never to do with any woman,' he said bitterly. His temper exploded. 'How *dare* you repay my trust by attempting to steal my son? How *dare* you try to separate me from him and deprive Harry of a father who loves him more than anything on this earth?'

'I wasn't going to go.' Desperation made her voice unsteady. 'I swear I'd changed my mind and I was going to turn the car around.'

He gave a grim laugh. 'There's no chance I'd believe a word you say. And there is even less chance that a court will award you custody of Harry after you were willing to risk his safety by taking him in the car when you are inexperienced at driving on roads in Spain.'

Cortez's voice was icy with disdain. 'My first opinion of you was correct and you are unfit to be his mother. The best place for Harry to be right now is in his nursery, safely asleep in his cot, and that is where I am going to take him.'

Elin beat her fists against the gates. She was crying so hard that she could barely speak. 'You seem to love Harry, but for how long will you love him?' she choked. 'When the novelty of fatherhood wears off will you lose interest in your child, the same as my adoptive father grew bored of me?'

She watched Cortez walk into the house and collapsed onto her knees in despair. Every ragged breath she dragged into her lungs hurt. 'If you take my son away from me you might as well cut my heart out,' she cried after him. 'He is all I have. *Please*.'

Violent rage coursed through Cortez. Elin should consider herself lucky that she was on the other side of the locked gates because if he could get his hands on her he'd be tempted to shake some sense into her.

But he would be tempted to do much more than shake her, he acknowledged with furious self-derision. Even though he had proof that she was an untrustworthy, deceitful bitch he still wanted her. She was a fever in his blood and a constant clamouring hunger in his gut. He thought about her all the time and there had been many nights in the past month when he'd resorted to using his hand to alleviate the throbbing ache of his arousal.

He resented the power she had over him. After Alandra he had assured himself that he would never allow a woman to affect him. But Elin had fooled him with her sweet smile, while all the time she had been plotting to steal his son. Ten years ago Alandra had told him that she did not want his baby and had ended her pregnancy. Sometimes when Cortez saw a child of roughly the same age as his child would have been he was still haunted by a deep sense of loss and regret. Now he had a son and he was fiercely determined that Elin would not deprive him of his right to be Harry's father.

In the nursery he carefully transferred Harry from the baby carrier to the cot. *'Te amo, mi hijo,'* he whispered as he leaned over the cot rail and kissed the baby's velvety soft cheek. Cortez hadn't known he could feel like this—so fiercely protective that he would kill anyone who tried to hurt his child. Harry needed his father, but he was not yet five months old and the inescapable truth was that he needed his mother too.

Cortez's jaw clenched when he walked over to the window that overlooked the driveway and saw Elin was where he had left her, slumped on her knees behind the locked gates. How long would she remain there? The answer felt like a punch in his gut. She would never abandon her son. Over and over again he had seen evidence of Elin's love for Harry. Her words echoed inside his head.

When the novelty of fatherhood wears off will you lose interest in your child, the same as my adoptive father grew bored of me?

Both he and Elin had suffered from Ralph Saunderson's failures as a father, Cortez brooded. Elin had not known her real parents, and although Ralph had adopted her and given her a home he had not given her the attention and love she had desperately needed. It was not hard to understand why Elin had trust issues. And he had not helped in that respect, Cortez acknowledged. *Dios*, he had taken her innocence and then turned his back on her. Cursing beneath his breath, he abruptly swung away from the window and took the device that operated the driveway gates from his pocket.

At first Elin couldn't understand what was happening when she suddenly fell forwards and landed on her face on the gravel driveway before she had a chance to put her hand out to save herself. The realisation that the gates had swung open sent relief flooding through her, and her legs trembled as she stumbled to her feet and ran towards the house. The front door was ajar and she tore across the hall and up the stairs to the nursery.

Her baby was fast asleep and blissfully unaware of the drama of the past half an hour. She clung to the side of the cot and forced herself to breathe deeply. Harry's long black lashes curled against his cheeks and his rosebud mouth was pursed in an adorable expression that brought more tears to Elin's eyes. If she had to crawl over broken glass to Cortez and plead with him not to seek custody of their son she would do whatever he demanded. She had better start by apologising, she thought ruefully.

His private suite was along the corridor. Her heart was thudding as she knocked on the door, and when there was no answer she cautiously stepped into the sitting room. Cortez wasn't there, nor in the adjoining master bedroom. Elin turned to leave, thinking he might be downstairs in his study. She froze when he emerged from the en suite bathroom.

He did not seem surprised to find her in his room

and flicked his cold gaze over her while Elin stared at him uncertainly, waiting for him to speak. His simmering silence ratcheted up her tension, but the shameful longing that the sight of Cortez always evoked in her licked fiery heat through her body and pooled, hot and molten, *there,* between her thighs, where only he had ever touched her.

He was naked apart from the towel wrapped around his hips, and droplets of water clung to his black chest hairs. She visualised the photo of him on Sancha's phone and all her feelings of hurt and anger exploded.

'How dare you say I am unfit to be Harry's mother? *I* have never left him to go off and spend a night with a lover.'

He frowned. 'Neither have I.'

'You went to Madrid, supposedly on business, and stayed with Sancha at the apartment you bought for her. She showed me a photo of you, naked in bed at your love nest. Sancha is your mistress, isn't she?'

Cortez did not deny it, and Elin felt sick. He walked past her into the sitting room and opened his briefcase that was on the table, returning to the bedroom moments later and handing her a piece of paper.

'What is this?' she muttered.

'The hotel receipt for the night that I stayed in Madrid.' He shrugged, and Elin could not help but notice the way his powerful shoulder muscles rippled beneath his bronzed satin skin. 'Sancha and I were lovers for a brief time but I ended my affair with her three months before I went to Cuckmere Hall for Ralph's funeral. My property portfolio includes an apartment block in Madrid and Teresa García asked me if I would rent a flat to her sister when Sancha was looking for a place to live.'

Elin noted that the date on the receipt tallied with the night when Cortez had stayed away. 'You could still have visited Sancha at her apartment.' And had sex with her, she thought, but did not voice her suspicion.

'I happened to run into her at a restaurant where I was having lunch with a client, but that's all,' he said calmly. 'I crammed two days of meetings into one day and worked until late so that I could come home, rather than have to spend another night away from you and Harry.'

It was scary how desperately she wanted to believe him. 'Then why did Sancha say that the photo of you on her phone was taken three weeks ago?'

'To cause trouble and make you jealous, I imagine. I broke up with her because she made it plain that she hoped I would marry her.'

'I am not *jealous*,' Elin denied, flushing hotly. Cortez sounded so matter-of-fact that she found she believed him. Sancha must have been bitter that he had dumped her, and Elin knew she had been too ready to believe the Spanish woman's spite because she was unsure of her own relationship with Cortez.

'You threatened to fight for custody of Harry,' she said in a low voice. 'But I don't want us to be embroiled in a court battle over our son. You were right to say that he needs both his parents, and so I… I want to go ahead with our wedding tomorrow.' In fact they were due to marry later today, she realised when she glanced at the clock and saw it was almost one a.m.

Elin didn't know how she'd expected Cortez to react. Not with a loud cheer, obviously, but she'd thought he would say *something*. He flicked his dark gaze over her once more and his implacable expression caused her heart to jolt against her ribs.

'You'll have to do better than that if you want to convince me that I should make you my wife,' he finally drawled.

'I don't understand.' She was fascinated by the glittering gold flecks in his eyes.

'If I hadn't caught you trying to sneak out of La Casa Jazmín, you would have stolen my son,' he said harshly. Elin's heart sank as she realised that he was still furious with her. 'You need to give me a good reason why I should marry you.'

She stared at him and wished he would put some clothes on because the sight of his near naked body was making it difficult for her to think straight. 'I don't know how to convince you,' she said helplessly.

He strolled over to the bed and sat down on the edge of the mattress. Elin's eyes were drawn to the towel he wore that rode up his thighs and barely concealed the bulge of his arousal. Angry and aroused were a dangerous combination, and she swallowed when her eyes crashed with his and she saw the speculative gleam in his unforgiving gaze.

'You can start by proving to me that you will be an obedient wife. Get undressed,' he commanded softly.

She was outraged by his arrogance, but at the same time she could not control the searing heat that swept through her and made every nerve ending in her body quiver. The truth was that she had secretly yearned for him to make love to her ever since he had brought her to Spain. When they had been out in public together he had acted the role of a loving and attentive fiancé, but when they were alone he had not made any attempt to seduce her after she'd agreed to marry him. She had believed Sancha because Cortez was such a virile man and surely he must have wanted sex in the weeks that they had been at La Casa Jazmín.

She wanted sex too, but not like this, with resentment and mistrust simmering between them. She could tell him to go to hell and retain her pride but risk the very real likelihood of losing custody of her baby. It wasn't a risk Elin was prepared to take.

Before she had attempted her ill-thought-out escape plan she'd changed into clothes that would be comfortable for travelling in with a small baby in tow. But her jeans were difficult to peel off when her hands were trembling. She felt the blush that stained her cheeks spread all the way down to her toes as she tugged her T-shirt over her head while Cortez watched her with an intent look in his eyes that made her stomach muscles contract.

If she had hoped for a reprieve she was disappointed. 'Why have you stopped?' he growled. 'Your plain underwear does not send me wild with desire. *If* I decide to marry you I will expect you to wear lingerie that excites me, not bores me.'

Once again she controlled the urge to tell him to go to hell. Only now did she realise how much damage she had done by betraying Cortez's trust. But she was not going to allow him to humiliate her, Elin decided as she reached behind her and unclipped her bra. She lifted her chin and held his gaze as she slid the straps down her arms, allowing the bra to fall to the floor.

She felt a little spurt of feminine triumph when dull colour flared on his magnificent cheekbones, and she was glad that her body had regained its pre-pregnancy shape with the help of regular sessions in the gym. Her stomach was flat, and although she'd always wished that her breasts were bigger, they were firm, and she saw Cortez's eyes focus on the hard points of her nipples that jutted provocatively forwards.

But he did not move; he just sat there waiting for her to finish unveiling her body to him. Elin wished she was wearing a sexy thong instead of her distinctly unglamorous underwear. No doubt he was used to seeing his mistresses in silk and lace. Temper made her movements jerky as she tugged her knickers down her legs and stepped out of them. She pushed her long hair over her shoulder and stared right back at him.

'I was a pretty child,' she told him. 'When a news crew filmed a piece about abandoned children at the bomb-damaged orphanage in Sarajevo, they turned the cameras on me because I was blonde and cute. I was lucky to be adopted by the Saundersons but there were many other children they could have chosen. Even at four years old I understood that I had been given a chance in life because of the way I looked.'

Cortez said nothing and his hard-boned features gave no clue to his thoughts. Elin felt a nervous flutter in the pit of her stomach when he lifted his hand and crooked his finger, beckoning her to him. She wanted to refuse him but she reminded herself that she wanted to keep her son. 'You only wanted my body,' she said flatly. 'And after you'd had me you walked away and did not give me another thought. You made me feel worthless.'

She caught her breath when he placed his hand on her stomach. His touch burned her and she knew he must have felt her muscles contract as awareness of his smouldering sensuality ripped through her.

'I wish I had seen you when your belly was swollen with our child,' he finally said and his voice was deeper than she had ever heard it, as if he felt as raw as she did. But that was impossible, Elin told herself. Cortez had demonstrated how unimportant she was to him when he'd failed to contact her for a year.

'You *should* have been around when Harry was born and I nearly died. I was terrified he would not have either of his parents,' she said thickly.

To her surprise he nodded. 'You're right; I should have been there for both of you.'

Something in his voice made Elin believe that his remorse was genuine and the tight bands around her heart loosened a little.

He lifted his other hand and shaped the curve of her hips and the indent of her waist before he moved his hands higher and splayed his fingers over her ribcage, tantalisingly close to the undersides of her breasts. She knew he could feel her erratic heart-beat and at that moment she hated him for the ease with which he could make her mindless with desire.

'Is there a purpose to this exercise?' she said grittily. 'Are you planning to throw me down on the bed and demonstrate your power over me by forcing me to have sex with you?'

He looked amused. 'Is that what you want me to do?'

'Of course not.' She silently cursed when she heard the huskiness in her voice. He was tying her in knots and he damned well knew it. Her stomach muscles clenched when he trailed his hand down her body and slid his fingers through the blonde curls at the junction between her thighs.

'Why did you try to run away with Harry?'

'I was worried you might grow bored of father-hood and abandon him.' *Like you abandoned me.* The unspoken words hung in the air between them.

He shook his head. 'I don't believe you. I've told you how much I wished I had a father when I was growing up, and I will always love and protect my son.'

Cortez slipped his hand between her legs, and Elin caught her breath when he eased his finger in-side her and discovered her molten heat. He gave a little tug of his hand to propel her forwards so that she was standing between his open legs.

'Our marriage cannot succeed without honesty. Tell me the truth, Elin.'

The truth! She gave a pained laugh and suddenly she was tired of fighting him, of fighting herself. 'The truth is that I'm scared of how you make me feel,' she muttered.

'How do I make you feel?' he demanded relent-lessly. He eased a second finger inside her and moved his hand in a devastating dance that left her incapable of concentrating on anything but the blissful sensa-tions he was creating.

She stared at his face, at his dark eyes flecked with gold and his beautiful mouth that could look stern or sensual depending on his mood. The smile that tugged the corners of his lips stole her heart and she had to remind herself that this was the man who had threatened to take her baby from her if she failed to persuade him to marry her.

'I told myself that the reason I slept with you at my birthday party was because I wasn't in control of my behaviour after my drink had been spiked with a date-rape drug. But the truth,' she whispered, 'is that I danced with many men that night and I didn't invite any of them into my bedroom. Only you. I saw you and you blew me away. But the next morning, when I woke and you had gone, I felt ashamed. When Virginia told me that her friend Tom had been charged with tampering with women's drinks, I pretended to myself that what had happened hadn't been my fault.'

She trembled as Cortez continued his erotic exploration of her body with his clever fingers. The way he was watching her intently while he pleasured her was shockingly intimate, and she closed her eyes as she moved against his hand.

'It was the same for me,' he growled. 'I took one look at you and I wanted you more than I'd wanted any other woman.'

Elin's eyelashes flew open and she gave him a startled look. 'In that case, why did you leave without waking me the next morning?'

'I was angry with myself. I'd read the tabloid stories about you and I couldn't understand why I had succumbed to your obvious charms. You were even more beautiful than the photos I'd seen of you, and you drove me out of my mind that night. But in the morning I was furious that you had made me lose control.'

Elin had seen evidence of how Cortez kept a tight

control on his emotions and she could imagine he had felt horrified by what he would have regarded as his weakness.

'Is that why you have kept your distance from me?' She wanted nothing more than to surrender to the mastery of his wickedly inventive fingers, but she fought against the tide of pleasure that she could feel building low in her pelvis.

He gave a husky laugh as he swirled his fingers inside her and she trembled. 'I'm not keeping my distance from you now, *querida*.'

'Because you're trying to teach me a lesson,' she choked. 'You don't want me.'

Cortez moved so fast that Elin couldn't have said how she came to be lying flat on her back on the bed with him on top of her. He had whipped off the towel from around his hips and she could feel the rock-hard length of his arousal between her legs. 'Does this feel like I don't want you?' he demanded hoarsely. 'You needed time to adjust. I will always be Harry's father and I'm not going to abandon you or him, ever.'

Of course everything Cortez did was for his son, Elin reminded herself. But she was finding it impossible to think clearly when she was trapped beneath him. And she'd been wrong in one respect, because the evidence that he desired her was unmistakable.

'I thought…' she began.

'Don't think, just feel,' he muttered as he bent his head to her breast and flicked his tongue across her nipple. He drew the swollen peak into his mouth and sucked hard until she writhed beneath him and he moved across to her other breast to mete out the same devastating punishment.

Elin ran her fingers through his hair, as she had longed to do often over the past few weeks. It felt like warm silk against her skin and when she explored the sculpted shape of his face the rough stubble on his jaw scraped her palm. Cortez lifted his head and stared down at her, the flecks in his dark eyes gleaming pure gold before he claimed her mouth in a kiss that plundered her soul.

Could he believe Elin? Cortez asked himself. Or was her admission that she'd tried to leave him because of the way he made her feel a lie to persuade him not to seek custody of their son? She had told him she would do anything to keep her baby, and perhaps this was all a lie—the soft gasps she gave when he twisted his fingers inside her, and the way she arched her slender body beneath him when he tasted her cherry-red nipples. But he found that he didn't care. All he cared about was that Elin was beneath him, and he pressed himself into the sweet contours of her body so that her breasts were crushed against his chest and her smooth thighs offered a tempting haven for his painfully hard erection.

But he forced himself to wait and ignore his primal instinct to drive his shaft deep inside her. He could not forget that if he hadn't happened to go into his study earlier, she might be carrying Harry onto a plane bound for England now. She'd said she had changed her mind and had been about to return to the house, but he did not know if he believed her and he was even less sure that he could trust her.

He'd played on Elin's fear that he might seek legal custody of Harry and told her she would have to convince him to marry her. But in truth he would never try to separate mother and child, and *he* needed to persuade *her* that marriage was not only in their son's best interest, but it would be good for her too.

She was not interested in his money. *Dios*, she had turned down thirty-five million pounds without hesitation. No, his trump card was Elin's obvious desire for him, Cortez brooded. Sexual chemistry had simmered between them since he had brought her to La Casa Jazmín, and he could see a double advantage to seducing her with sex. He would use every skill he possessed as a lover to bind her to him so that she would never want to leave and take their son, and at the same time he would sate himself on her exquisite body until the damnable hold she had over him was broken.

He stretched out next to her on the bed and propped himself up on one elbow while he skimmed his other hand over her delectable curves and felt a tremor run through her when he cupped her breast. Her body betrayed her beautifully. Her nipples were flushed and damp from where he had sucked them, and the musky feminine fragrance of her desire stirred his senses when he nudged her thighs apart with his shoulders and placed his mouth over the delicate nub of her clitoris.

She gave a startled cry. 'You can't…'

'Oh, but I can,' he assured her softly and bent his head to continue his task of exploring her with his tongue. He loved that she was shocked by the intimate caress and at the same time he was appalled by the fierce possessiveness he felt. She had told him she'd been a virgin when they had slept together at her birthday party, and he believed her despite the stories about her supposed torrid love-life reported in the tabloids. Her innocent delight in what he was doing to her was coupled with surprised gasps that could only be genuine.

'*Cortez.*' She breathed his name like a prayer, a plea, and her guttural voice told him what her body was already signalling to him as she bucked and writhed and sobbed beneath his merciless onslaught. He considered making her come with his mouth, but his own need was too great. He was shocked to realise that his control was slipping and his plan to enslave Elin with sex could go spectacularly wrong.

Somehow he held back long enough to slide a protective sheath over his erection, and then he thrust his way inside her and heard above the thunderous pounding of his heart the harsh groan he made when he sank into her velvet heat and discovered heaven. Somewhere along the path to nirvana the seducer had become the seduced and the slave master was now the slave. And the most astonishing thing was Cortez did not care that the point of making love to Elin was to trap her in his sensual web. He simply wanted to worship her and glory in the knowledge that she was his.

He set a rhythm and drove into her with steady strokes that quickly took them both to the edge. She filled up his senses with the fragrance of her skin when he pressed his lips to her throat, and the sweet taste of her lips when he kissed her mouth. He captured her cry as she suddenly arched beneath him and her body trembled like a slender bow under intolerable tension, seconds before she climaxed around him. And when he thrust deep into her for a final time and felt the unstoppable force of his own release thunder through him, she filled up his heart utterly and exclusively. *His*.

CHAPTER TEN

IT FELT AS if she were watching a replay of a bad film, Elin thought when she opened her eyes and discovered that her room was filled with bright sunshine and she was alone in bed. Just like the morning after her birthday party in London over a year ago, she ached *everywhere*. Erotic memories of Cortez's hands and mouth—dear God, his wicked mouth—caressing every inch of her body, flooded her mind, and pain filled her heart.

Last night they had made love endlessly in his big bed, until the sky outside the window had turned the palest pink as the sun edged above the horizon. She had fallen into an exhausted sleep in Cortez's arms but, although she had no recollection of him doing so, he must have carried her back to her bedroom before he'd left her—again.

Her heart leapt when the door opened, but plummeted when a maid entered the room. Rosa was followed by another housemaid, Maria, and the two girls were giggling as they carried a large flat box and deposited it on the bed.

'Your wedding dress,' Rosa told Elin in reply to her puzzled look. 'From Señor Ramos,' the maid added helpfully.

Elin hastily pulled her robe around her naked body that bore the marks of Cortez's lovemaking. The rough stubble on his jaw had grazed her breasts and her inner thighs. She determinedly shut off her wayward thoughts as she opened the box and lifted a dress out from the layers of tissue. It was an exquisitely simple sheath made of pure white silk, exactly the style of wedding dress she would have chosen if she'd been a real bride. But for her sham marriage to Cortez she had bought a pale blue skirt and jacket that could best be described as functional. Did he hope she would wear the unashamedly romantic dress?

Her heart was beating fast as she turned her attention to the other boxes the maids had brought to her room. One box contained a pair of pretty, strappy white shoes. She took the lid off another to reveal delicate lingerie as fine as gossamer. Maria opened the final box and held up a bouquet of white roses, each half-opened flower so perfect and pure that tears filled Elin's eyes.

Her phone rang and Cortez greeted her, his voice as dark and indulgent as the finest bittersweet chocolate. 'Good morning, *querida*. I don't want to panic you but we are due to get married in one hour.'

'I…' She broke off as she glanced down at her hand and saw her engagement ring that she had left in his study before she'd planned to leave La Casa Jazmín the previous night twinkling on her finger. 'When did you return my ring?'

'I slipped it back onto your finger before I left you to sleep for a couple of hours, having kept you awake for most of the night,' he said drily. 'It is meant to be bad luck for the bride and groom to see each other before the wedding.' He paused and then said softly, 'I would like the omens for our marriage to be good. The maids will help you to get ready, and the nanny is back from her trip and has taken charge of Harry.'

With a stab of guilt, Elin realised that she had not thought of her son until that moment. But when she hurried into the nursery Barbara shooed her back to her room after she'd given Harry a cuddle. There was just enough time for her to shower, blow-dry her hair and apply minimal make-up before the maids slipped the wedding dress over her head. It was a perfect fit, and the cool silk felt deliciously sensual against her skin.

She'd assumed Cortez would be waiting for her and they would travel to the Town Hall in Jerez together for the civil ceremony. But when she went downstairs she was met by the butler, who told her that Señor Ramos had already departed for the wedding venue and had taken Harry with him. Reality cast a shadow over Elin's excitement with the realisation that he did not trust her. Last night he had made love to her with passion coupled with unexpected tenderness that had given her hope for their relationship. But this morning his message was clear. He had laid claim to his son. Cortez would not force her to marry him, and it was her decision whether or not she met him at the Town Hall.

It was a stark choice. Marry a man who did not love her, or lose custody of her baby and be denied her chance to own a share of Saunderson's Wines. If the marriage failed she would at least have a means of supporting herself and Harry with the winery business. Her footsteps did not falter as she walked out of La Casa Jazmín and climbed into the car that was waiting to take her to her wedding.

She supposed Cortez had arranged for her to wear a wedding dress and carry a bouquet of flowers to convince the wedding guests that their marriage was real. But when she stepped out of the limousine and walked into the Town Hall he was waiting to escort her into the marriage room, and she noticed a nerve jump in his cheek that almost made her think he was as nervous as she was. He looked devastatingly handsome in a light grey suit and blue silk tie, and the expression in his eyes when he saw her made Elin's heart miss a beat.

'You look just as I imagined you would do in that dress,' he said huskily. 'Pure and innocent and incomparably beautiful.'

Some of her tension lifted and she dimpled at him. 'I'm not quite so innocent after last night, but I very much enjoyed being corrupted by you.' Amazing sex was a good start for their marriage, she thought prosaically, and perhaps in time Cortez would grow to care for her.

The gold flecks in his dark eyes gleamed. 'You say this to me now, moments before I will have to stand in front of the celebrant and our guests and pray they cannot tell that I have an erection as hard as a rock? I will take my retribution tonight, *querida*,' he warned her softly, sending a shiver of anticipation through her.

'I'm counting on it,' she murmured and hid a smile when he swore beneath his breath as he placed his arm possessively around her waist and led her towards the marriage celebrant.

It had been an unexpectedly joyous day, Elin thought much later, after she had made her vows in a voice that shook a little, and Cortez had made his in an oddly fierce tone that echoed the intent expression in his eyes when the celebrant had told him he could kiss his bride.

Harry was the centre of attention at the reception lunch which was held at La Casa Jazmín for the twenty or so wedding guests, who included Nic and Teresa García, but not Teresa's sister Sancha. The only thing that slightly marred Elin's happiness was the absence of her brother. Jarek had been adamant that he was too busy with his job at Saunderson's Bank in Japan to be able to take time off to attend the wedding, even though she had told him how much she wanted him to be there.

Elin hated the distance that had grown between

them. She understood her brother's bitterness towards Ralph Saunderson's heir, and she was worried that Jarek believed she had betrayed him by marrying Cortez. The last few times she had phoned him, he had sounded as if he was drunk, and she feared he was sliding deeper into the dark place in his mind where she knew he was haunted by memories of the past.

She pushed her concerns about Jarek to the back of her mind as she watched Cortez proudly showing off his son. After Harry's birth, when she had haemorrhaged badly, her terrible fear had been that if she died, her baby would be placed in an orphanage. Now her son had his father and she knew that Cortez would be a million times a better father than Ralph Saunderson had been.

Harry's future was secure, and as for her own future—she looked over at her husband and found him watching her. The glint in Cortez's gaze made her wish they were alone so that he could make love to her. When she was in his arms his fierce passion made her forget that their marriage was a practical arrangement and she could pretend that he loved her as deeply as she now accepted that she loved him.

After lunch Cortez drove Elin, Harry and the nanny to the airport, where his private jet was waiting. 'If you had told me we were going abroad, I would have changed out of my wedding dress,' she muttered, feeling self-conscious when she had to walk through the busy airport terminal in her wedding gown.

'I have spent all day anticipating undressing my beautiful bride,' he drawled. 'Allow me to enjoy my fantasy for a few more hours until we reach our destination.'

He refused to tell Elin where they were heading, but by early evening, when the plane prepared to land at a small airport in West Sussex, she gave him a half hopeful, half disbelieving look. 'Are we going to spend our honeymoon at Cuckmere Hall? I thought you hated the house? You called it an ugly Gothic monstrosity.'

'I'm willing to re-evaluate my opinion of it, for your sake. I know how much you love the place.' He shrugged. 'I think perhaps I hated Cuckmere because it represented everything that Ralph had denied my mother. If she'd had an easier life maybe she would not have died far too young. Harry is Ralph's grandson and I have a responsibility to care for the estate and provide good leadership at the bank so that one day our son can take over from me. Which reminds me,' he added. 'Now we are married you will have to re-register Harry's birth so that I can be declared his natural father on the birth record.'

The infant heir to Cuckmere Hall seemed unimpressed when the car drew up outside the house and Cortez carried his son into the house. Harry wanted to be fed and demonstrated his excellent lung capacity by yelling loudly until the nanny took him upstairs to the nursery. Meanwhile, Elin explored the familiar rooms that had been updated with a fresh décor by an interior designer company that Cortez had hired.

'I have resigned from my position as CEO of Hernandez Bank in Spain,' he told Elin. 'I've also appointed an operations manager to oversee Felipe & Cortez, to give me time to concentrate on running Saunderson's Bank. It means that we can alternate between living here at Cuckmere Hall and at La Casa Jazmín. When Harry is school age we'll decide then whether to make our home in England or Spain.'

The housekeeper had laid out a light supper for them in the conservatory overlooking the garden, and Baines served a vintage Saunderson's sparkling wine before he retired and left them alone.

'Home,' Elin said softly. 'Cuckmere represents safety,' she explained to Cortez. 'Before I was adopted and came to live here, I remember feeling scared when the orphanage was bombed. But at least I had Jarek to take care of me.' She sighed. 'My brother refuses to discuss the past. I wish he was able to talk about what happened when Sarajevo was attacked. He let slip once that he used to earn money by taking food to the Bosnian soldiers on the front line, and then he would buy food for the children who had been abandoned in the wreckage of the orphanage. I know he has nightmares about the things he saw when he was a boy, and also about when Mama was killed.'

'What exactly happened to Lorna Saunderson?'

'She was shot dead by an armed raider during a

bungled robbery at a jewellers.' Elin's voice wobbled as memories of that devastating day flooded her mind. 'Jarek and I had taken Mama to choose a present for her birthday. The raider said in court that he hadn't meant to fire the gun, but he panicked and when the gun went off Mama was killed instantly. My brother blames himself for not saving her life. He can't accept that there was nothing he could have done.'

She bit her lip, wondering how much she could reveal to Cortez without betraying her brother. 'Jarek really struggled afterwards, and there was a period when he drank a little too much and spent more time than was good for him in casinos and nightclubs. His relationship with Ralph had always been difficult and it got a lot worse. I pretended to be an out of control party girl to distract the paparazzi's attention away from my brother because I was afraid Ralph might sack him from Saunderson's Bank.'

She took a sip of wine and felt a pang of sadness that Mama would never taste the wine produced from the vines she had planted. To her surprise, Cortez reached across the table and took her hand in his.

'I understand how much you must miss Lorna,' he said gently. 'After my mother died, my grief made me a little crazy for a while.'

She gave him a startled look. 'I can't imagine you ever losing control of your emotions.'

'I did once, and paid a heavy price for my weakness.' Cortez's voice was suddenly harsh and Elin sensed that he had revealed more about himself to her than he'd intended.

He took a sip from his glass. 'This is an excellent wine,' he said, making an obvious attempt to steer the conversation away from his personal life. 'By marrying me you have fulfilled the terms of Ralph's will and you own fifty per cent of Saunderson's Wines. I am keen to work in partnership with you to develop the winery. Do you want to tell me your plans for the business?'

'For a start, I'd like to expand the vineyard and plant another four or five hectares of vines.' Elin jumped up and walked to the door of the conservatory. 'Come with me and I'll show you what I'm thinking of. What's wrong?' she asked when he looked amused.

'I can't imagine many *vigneronnes* inspect their vines wearing a wedding dress.'

She shrugged. 'I could go and change, but I thought you have been fantasising about taking my dress off later.'

His eyes gleamed with wicked intent. 'Not a lot later,' he warned. 'I can't wait much longer to fulfil several of my fantasies, including the one where…' He bent his head close to her ear and whispered what he would like to do to her.

Elin's cheeks were still pink when she led Cortez across the garden. They walked through the Cuckmere estate to the vineyards that she had helped her adoptive mother to plant on the chalky slopes of the South Downs. The vines were covered in green leaves and clusters of grape berries which would continue to grow over the summer until the ripened fruit was harvested in September.

Now, in late May, the summer equinox was only a few weeks away and dusk fell late as the days lengthened. In the gloaming the white flowers on the hawthorn bushes looked like tiny stars and their perfume mingled with the sweet scent of wild honeysuckle. The air was soft and still, disturbed only by the bleating of the sheep that grazed on the Downs, and by Elin's voice as she outlined her vision for the estate winery.

She slipped her shoes off, enjoying the feel of the soft grass beneath her feet as she strolled with Cortez among the rows of vines. He listened intently to her ideas, occasionally asking a question or making a suggestion. When she finally ran out of breath and words, he smiled. 'I'm impressed by your enthusiasm to expand the business. We'll do it.'

'It will require significant financial investment,' she said cautiously. 'This is my dream, Cortez. Do you really believe we could make Saunderson's Wines into a major UK wine producer?'

'I believe in you,' he murmured. 'With your extensive knowledge of viticulture and your drive and determination, I don't see how you can fail.'

Elin was tempted to point out that growing grapes in England's unpredictable climate did not have the guaranteed success that Cortez was used to in the near-perfect conditions of dry, warm southern Spain. But she was overwhelmed by his confidence in her. After Mama had died, Ralph had lost all interest in the estate winery and had refused to take Elin's ideas for expanding the business seriously. But she was convinced that with Cortez's support Saunderson's Wines could produce a world-class wine.

She halted halfway along a row of vines and turned to face him. 'I like the idea of us working together in partnership. I was wondering whether you see yourself as a sleeping partner, or if you will take an active role?' she said innocently.

His soft growl of laughter curled around her and desire coiled tight and urgent in her belly as he slid his hand beneath the weight of her hair and drew her towards him. 'I envisage that my participation will be *very* active,' he told her. His warm breath grazed her lips before he claimed her mouth and kissed her with a fierce hunger that made her melt against him. 'Naturally, I will welcome any input you might like to make to our partnership.'

'Is this the sort of input you mean?' she whispered, dipping her tongue into his mouth.

'Exactly like that, *querida*.' Cortez's tone was no longer teasing, but raw with sexual need. Elin ran her hands over his chest and felt the erratic thud of his heart. She continued her exploration and brushed her fingers along the hard ridge of his arousal she could feel beneath his trousers, making him groan.

It thrilled her to know that she did this to him. She

undid his zip and he muttered something in Spanish, but he did not try to stop her when she freed his thickened length from his clothes and stretched her hand around him. Steel encased in velvet. So powerful and yet so sensitive, she discovered when she gripped him harder and he shuddered.

She had been afraid that Cortez might try to undermine her once she was his wife, but instead he had brought her back to the home she loved and offered her a business partnership. Now it was her turn to prove that she wanted to be an equal partner in all areas of their relationship, Elin thought as she knelt in front of him. She did not have the courage to tell him she loved him, but she could show him.

If this was a dream, Cortez never wanted to wake up. The moon had risen in the night sky, and it cast a silvery gleam over Elin's upturned face as she sank gracefully to her knees before him and rested her cheek on his thigh. Her long hair poured like a golden river down her back and felt like silk against his fingers when he placed his hand at the back of her head. He couldn't believe she actually intended to fulfil his hottest fantasy. Just the sight of her in her white silk dress that became semi-transparent in the moonlight was better than any erotic dream he'd had about her—and he'd had plenty.

She flicked her tongue over his swollen tip and he rocked back on his heels while his heart tried to claw its way out of his chest. *Dios*, this must be a dream and he would rather die than wake up before it reached its climax.

'Elin,' he growled, trying to fight his longing for her to lick him again. He swallowed convulsively and ordered himself to take control of the situation. After Alandra he had promised himself that he would never give a woman power over him. But here he was, in the most vulnerable position a man could be, at Elin's mercy, and the mercy of her tongue that she was using with such devastating effect.

She lifted her head away from him and he did not know whether to be relieved or disappointed. She looked like an angel kneeling there, and her soft smile shattered his resolve to end this madness. Maybe it was a dream, he consoled himself when she closed her lips around his shaft and her hair fell around her face like a golden veil.

The feel of her mouth on him drove him to the edge of reason. But, more than his physical response to her, he was moved by her generosity and eagerness to please him after he had blackmailed her to marry him by threatening to seek custody of their son. He hoped their marriage would be a true partnership and what he wanted more than anything was to make love to his wife.

He drew her to her feet and kissed her mouth, slow and sweet beneath the stars and the silver moon. She kissed him back with that generosity of hers that made him ache right down to his soul. If this was a dream, he never wanted it to end, he thought as he finally did what he had dreamed of doing all day and slid the white silk wedding dress over her shoulders to reveal her slender body. He removed the wisps of silk and lace lingerie and bared her small, perfect breasts with their rosy tips.

The dew-damp grass was cool on his back when he lay down and held her against his chest. He heard her catch her breath when he guided her down onto him, and she paused for a moment while her body adjusted to the thrust of his hard length inside her. He wrapped his hands in her hair and kissed her rose-tipped breasts as she moved above him—a pale nymph, ethereal and lovely in the moonlight. And when they soared to the stars together and she cried out his name, he dared to believe that the dream would last for ever.

He should have known dreams were ephemeral. Reality caught up with Cortez four weeks later, and it started with an earthquake in Japan.

CHAPTER ELEVEN

'ARE WE STILL on our honeymoon, or is this real life?' Elin asked Cortez one morning, midway through the fourth week of their marriage.

He placed the tray he had carried up to their room on the bedside table and sat down on the bed, bending his head to kiss her. It was a long kiss and Elin was breathless when he finally, and with obvious reluctance, lifted his mouth from hers. 'Does there have to be a difference?' he murmured.

The aroma of freshly brewed coffee rose from the cafetière. Elin picked up the pale pink rose that was lying on the tray and inhaled its sensual fragrance. 'I only ask because you have brought me a rose from the garden every morning since we came to Cuckmere Hall. I've decided that I like being married,' she confessed, feeling inexplicably shy. Inexplicable, because he knew every centimetre of her body and had revealed a sensual side to her nature that delighted both of them.

Being married to Cortez was nothing short of wonderful. Bringing her a rose every day was just one of so many ways he made her feel cherished. Their relationship might have had a rocky start, but these past weeks had been the happiest of her life and it was hard to remember that theirs was a marriage of convenience to allow them to both be full-time parents to their son.

Maybe the reason why they had married didn't matter, Elin mused. She felt that she and Cortez were growing closer every day. She loved spending time with him and Harry as a family, but she also loved the times when they were alone together, working in the vineyard and winery, chatting over dinner or relaxing in the evening and watching a film before they went to bed. She especially loved being in bed with him and they could lose themselves in their private world of passion that was stronger than ever.

'Tell me what in particular you like about our marriage,' he said in his molten chocolate voice that she found as irresistible as the rest of him. She cupped his face in her hands and whispered in his ear all the things she liked him to do to her, and all the things that she liked doing to him.

'You have a wicked mind, Señora Ramos,' he growled. 'Hold on to the thought about the whipped cream until I come home.'

Elin finally registered the fact that he was dressed in a suit instead of jeans and a polo shirt that she'd grown used to seeing him wearing at Cuckmere.

'I need to go to work occasionally,' he said, kissing away her frown. 'I'll stay up in London for the rest of the week. I haven't been as involved at Saunderson's Bank as I should have been because you are a dangerous distraction. Fortunately, the bank has a good management team, but Andrew Fowler, the COO, called me early this morning and requested an urgent meeting at the London head office.'

'Is there a problem at the bank?'

'Andrew didn't say much.' It was Cortez's turn to frown. 'Your brother seems to have gone AWOL from the Japanese office again. Have you spoken to Jarek recently?'

Elin shook her head. 'I haven't heard from him since before our wedding.' She unconsciously chewed on her lower lip. 'It's unusual for him not to call me, and he hasn't responded to any of my calls or text messages. I'm worried about him,' she admitted.

'Hey,' he said softly, 'I'm sure your brother is fine.' Cortez slid his hand beneath her chin and tilted her face up to his. He dropped a light kiss on the tip of her nose before taking his phone from his jacket pocket.

'In answer to your question of whether we are still on our honeymoon. The answer is yes, and this is where we will spend the next two weeks.' A picture of a French château came onto his phone screen. 'Château Giraud is in the Dordogne region of France and has well established vineyards and a winery. I thought we could explore the ancient caves nearby, and the heated pool in the château's grounds will be perfect to introduce Harry to swimming.'

He stood up and walked across the room to the bureau. 'I'd actually arranged a couple of meetings at the bank before Andrew Fowler called me. Knowing that I would be in London, I made an appointment at the passport office to get a replacement passport for Harry under his new name. I'll need to take our marriage certificate and his birth certificate with me.'

Cortez lifted a document out of a drawer in the bureau and frowned as he looked at it. 'You said you would re-register Harry's birth and name me as his natural father on the birth record, as the law requires. But this is his original birth certificate, which states that his name is Saunderson and does not include my details.'

Elin sat up and pushed her hair out of her eyes. The accusatory tone of Cortez's voice made her flush guiltily. 'I forgot all about it,' she admitted. 'I meant to download the necessary form and take it to the register office, but it completely slipped my mind.'

'Are you sure that is the reason?' Cortez stood at the foot of the bed and subjected her to a hard stare that made her feel like a naughty child.'

'Of course.' She heard the defensive note in her voice. 'What other reason do you think there could be?'

His dark eyes bored into her, cold and hard without the golden flecks that usually gleamed with warmth. 'You know it is important to me that I am recognised as Harry's father on a legal document. Only you can re-register his birth to include my details. But maybe it suits you if I am not named as his father on the birth record,' he suggested tersely.

'I'm human and I forget things occasionally,' Elin

snapped, her temper stirring in response to Cortez's clipped voice. But she felt uncomfortable as she acknowledged there was a grain of truth in what he had said. She hadn't got round to changing the details on Harry's birth certificate because subconsciously she'd thought that if her marriage to Cortez failed she would automatically be granted custody of her son.

She glanced at the rose that Cortez had brought from the garden for her and her guilty feeling intensified. 'I'll sort out the paperwork to have your name added to Harry's birth record today,' she promised.

He nodded but although he returned her smile the expression in his eyes was still guarded. Elin sensed his tension when she knelt up on the bed and placed her hands on his shoulders so that she could cover his mouth with hers. The incident made her realise that the contentment they had both discovered in their marriage was fragile.

She missed him as soon as she heard his car roar away down the drive. Trust needed to be on both sides, she acknowledged. Cortez had shown her over the past weeks since their wedding that she could trust him. Why, he had even brought her to Cuckmere Hall, which he had once described as a Gothic monstrosity.

The argument was the first time that they had fallen out during their marriage, and it was her fault, Elin thought dismally. She was determined to make it up to him, and when Harry had settled down for his afternoon nap she switched on the computer in Cortez's study and filled out an online form, and then made an appointment at the local register office to arrange for both of Harry's parents' details to be included on his birth certificate.

Her phone rang and relief swept through her when she heard her brother's voice. 'I've been trying to contact you ever since you missed my wedding,' she told him. 'Where are you? Cortez said you haven't been seen at the Japanese office for a few days.'

'I'm not in Japan… I'm in London. Elin…' Jarek sounded tense '…have you heard about the earthquake in Japan?'

'Oh, my God! I haven't seen any news reports today. Are you all right?'

'I'm fine. I actually flew back to London two days ago, so I wasn't affected by the earthquake. At least, not physically.'

Something about her brother's tone made Elin uneasy. 'What do you mean?'

'I can't explain now. Is Cortez there? I need to speak to him.'

'He went to Saunderson's Bank in London this morning. The COO asked to see him urgently. Jarek, what has happened?' she asked worriedly when her brother swore. 'Are you in some kind of trouble?'

'That's one way of putting it.' His tone was grim.

'Why can't you tell me? We have always confided in each other.' It hurt her to realise that a chasm had opened up between her and her brother since she had married Cortez. When they were children in Sarajevo Jarek had risked his life for her many times, and she owed him her loyalty.

'You can't help me, *ijubljen*,' Jarek said flatly. His use of the Bosnian endearment that he had often used when she was a little girl tugged on Elin's emotions.

'I'll support you, no matter what the problem is,' she assured him fiercely. 'Are you at your apartment? I'll come now.' She remembered that the nanny was away visiting relatives. 'I'll put Harry in the car and drive up to town to meet you. Cortez is going to be in London for a couple of days and he doesn't need to know that I've spoken to you.'

She heard a sound behind her and glanced across the room. Her heart missed a beat when she saw Cortez standing in the doorway, and she wondered if he had realised that she was talking to her brother. 'I have to go,' she muttered to Jarek before quickly ending the call.

'I didn't expect you back so soon.' She smiled at Cortez but his expression was unreadable.

'Evidently.' He stepped into the study and closed the door behind him. 'I take it that was Jarek you were speaking to?'

'I...yes.' Elin realised there was no point denying it.

His lip curled cynically. 'How curious that your brother, who you told me you hadn't heard from for weeks, was in contact with you once I had left Cuckmere Hall.' A nerve jumped in his cheek. 'I heard you say that you are going to meet Jarek and take Harry with you.' He stalked towards her, his dark eyes glinting with fury that made Elin back away from him. 'Over my dead body,' he snarled. 'I won't allow you to take my son from me.'

'I wasn't...' she began.

He cut off the rest of her words with a bitter laugh. 'Even now you look and sound like an innocent angel, and it proves that I am a fool for wanting to believe in you. 'Tell me, *querida*—' he made the endearment sound like a curse '—were you planning to help your brother escape abroad? The three of you would disappear some place where I couldn't find you? It makes sense now why you did not include me on Harry's birth certificate or change the details on his passport.'

'I told you I simply forgot to add your name on his birth record,' she insisted, but Cortez ignored her.

'I rushed back here when I heard news reports of an earthquake in Japan. No one had been able to get hold of your brother, and I guessed you would be worried about him. But you must have known he had returned to England, just as you knew all along what he was doing at the bank in Japan.'

'You're not making any sense.' Elin's spine was jammed against the desk, but when she tried to step around Cortez he grabbed hold of her wrist. 'Ow! You're hurting me. Why would Jarek need to escape abroad?'

'*Dios!* Stop pretending you don't know what your brother has been doing for the last few months.' His explosion of temper made Elin flinch. 'You are in Jarek's confidence and you must have been aware of his irregular trading practices at Saunderson's Bank.

Technically, he did not do anything illegal, but he took unacceptable risks with the bank's funds by using his position as a derivatives broker to speculate on the future direction of the Japanese markets.'

Cortez raked his hair off his brow and glared at Elin. 'A few months ago Jarek's unhedged losses began to accumulate, but he might still have pulled off his gamble if there hadn't been a large earthquake in Japan this morning. The effect on the Asian financial markets was catastrophic and, as a safeguard, trading on the Nikkei was temporarily stopped. The value of Jarek's investments plummeted. So far he has lost Saunderson's Bank one hundred million pounds and the situation is likely to get worse over the next few days.'

Elin swallowed. No wonder Jarek had sounded strained on the phone.

'If I had been more involved at the bank these past weeks I might have noticed discrepancies in Jarek's daily trading reports. But you cleverly held my attention here at Cuckmere,' Cortez said bitterly. He let go of her wrist as if he could not bear to touch her. 'You used all your feminine wiles to keep me hooked on you and distract my attention away from what your brother was up to.'

She felt sick when she realised he was deadly serious. 'I don't have any feminine wiles,' she said shakily.

He gave another mirthless laugh that sliced through her heart like a rapier. 'You went down on your knees in front of me and gifted me such sweet pleasure that you made me think…' He broke off and stared at her with bitter contempt. There was no flicker of emotion on his granite-hard face as he watched her tears slide down her cheeks.

'I swear I had no idea what my brother was doing, and I certainly did not make love to you with an ulterior motive. I don't know how you could believe I would do that,' Elin choked. She was devastated by Cortez's accusations and horrified by what her brother had done. But she was not only agonisingly hurt, she was as angry as hell.

'We seem to have come full circle,' she told Cortez bitterly. 'On the day of Ralph's funeral you refused to believe that Harry was your son. And you accused me of being a drug-user without any real evidence. I thought I had finally earned your trust but you are still determined to think the worst of me. I can only repeat that I did not know about Jarek's risky trading strategy at the bank.'

'Do you deny that you were planning to take Harry and go and meet your brother?'

'No… I don't deny it. I wanted to find out what was wrong with Jarek. I was going to take Harry with me because Barbara is on annual leave, but I would have returned to Cuckmere Hall. I have already emailed the form to effect the changes to Harry's birth record and include you as his father. You can check my email account if you don't believe me,' she said, pointing to the computer. But Cortez swung away from her and strode over to the door.

'I don't believe a word in your pretty, lying head,'

he said savagely. 'Years ago I was denied my child by a woman who lied to me repeatedly, and I swore I would never be so stupid to trust any woman again. I almost broke my vow with you, Elin, but I won't be a fool again.'

She was stunned by his revelation about his past and only when she heard a door slam shut did she run out into the hall. By the time she had opened the front door Cortez was climbing into his car. 'Where are you going?'

'To deal with your brother,' he replied ominously. 'Don't even think of leaving Cuckmere and taking Harry because I swear I will find you—and you'll wish I hadn't.'

He fired the engine and as the car began to roll down the drive Elin ran alongside it, clinging on to the open window. 'I don't know what Jarek has done but I'm sure there will be an explanation. He hasn't been in a good place since Mama died, and I admit I should have told you about his issues,' she panted as she tried to keep up with the moving car. 'Why would I plan to go away with my brother when you have given me everything I could possibly want?'

'I forced you into marriage by threatening to try and take your baby away from you.' There was a hollowness in Cortez's voice that made her heart ache.

'I don't remember you dragging me to our wedding. I chose to marry you, not because of Harry, or because it allowed me to claim my inheritance...'

They had almost reached the bottom of the driveway and Elin's hand fell away from the car.

'What possible other reason could you have for marrying me?' he demanded.

Nothing but her complete honesty would do, and she was afraid she had left it too late. *'I love you.'*

The car came to an abrupt halt and he stared at her for what seemed like eternity before his mouth twisted in a cynical smile. 'That is the biggest lie of all,' he said harshly before he accelerated away so fast that the tyres screeched.

Cortez was glad that the traffic heading into London was busy because it meant he had to concentrate on driving and not allow his thoughts to stray to Elin. A pack of reporters were gathered outside Saunderson's Bank's headquarters. The news of huge financial losses to the bank and speculation about the future of Saunderson's was already in the media. He gave a short statement which contained few facts, but most journalists did not care about facts and no doubt the papers tomorrow would carry dramatic headlines about the bank that bore little in the way of truth, he thought sardonically.

Truth and lies. Right from the start, his opinion of Elin had been formed by what he had read about her in the tabloids. But she had proved over and over again that she was nothing like the selfish, self-absorbed It Girl she was portrayed by the paparazzi. He had accused her of lying to him—but what if he had misjudged her *again*?

He chaired a crisis meeting with the board and put out a statement to the shareholders that all steps were being taken to limit the damage to Saunderson's Bank. But, although he was facing the greatest professional crisis of his career, Cortez realised that he didn't give a damn about anything but Elin and the abominable way he had treated her. How the hell could she love him? he asked himself grimly. Surely she must have lied about that.

When his office door opened he thought it probable that the only person who looked more haggard than he did was Elin's brother. He had planned exactly what he would say to Jarek before he sacked him and called Security to escort him from Saunderson's Bank. But Cortez had finally got his priorities in order.

'Elin explained that she suffered a near fatal blood loss after giving birth, and while she was in Intensive Care you stayed with Harry and refused to leave him.' He swallowed hard as he acknowledged his guilt that he should have been with Elin throughout her pregnancy and their son's birth. He could never forgive himself for abandoning her. 'I am in your debt,' he told Jarek, 'for being there for my son and for Elin.'

A flicker of surprise and grudging respect flared in Jarek's ice-blue eyes that rarely showed any emotion. 'My sister means the world to me,' he said curtly. 'She had nothing to do with the bloody mess I've caused. If she'd had any clue about the financial risks I was taking at the bank she would have tried to persuade me to tell you. Elin is the most honest, loyal person in the world.'

It was what Cortez had been afraid of. He had chosen to believe the worst about Elin because then he could assure himself that all he felt for her was sexual attraction. Her brother had confirmed what he had known deep down for a long time, and the realisation that he was a coward made him feel even worse about himself, if that were possible.

He looked intently at his brother-in-law. 'The only reason I'm prepared to give you a second chance is because Elin adores you. What are you going to do about the goddamned mess you've created at the bank?'

'I give you my word that I'll sort the problem out,' Jarek said with his trademark cool arrogance. 'I'll repay the bank every penny of the money I lost.'

'No more taking risks.'

'I can't promise that.' Elin's brother pushed his long dirty-blond hair out of his eyes. 'Sometimes risk is necessary if you want to reap the richest reward.'

There was only one reward he wanted, Cortez thought with sudden, blinding insight. He was prepared to risk everything he owned, including his heart, for a chance of a lifetime of happiness.

He shot to his feet so fast that Jarek looked startled. 'I too have something to sort out,' Cortez said gruffly. 'I only hope I haven't left it too late.'

It was raining. Hard. The heatwave had come to an abrupt end with a violent thunderstorm, and Elin, who had been in the vineyard without a jacket, was drenched. She could have run back to the house to get out of the rain, but she simply did not have the energy and she trudged up the driveway with her head bowed against the downpour.

The previous afternoon she'd watched Cortez drive away from Cuckmere Hall. She'd felt furious that he had accused her unjustly *again*, and she'd lugged her clothes out of the master suite that she'd shared with him, back to her old bedroom. She had ordered herself not to cry. Surely she'd shed enough tears over a man who had proved time and again that he had a heart of stone. She'd definitely wasted enough time loving a man who would never return her love.

But, lying in her lonely bed, memories had crept into her mind of Cortez greeting her every morning with a rose he had picked from the garden, and she'd wept so hard that her heart might have broken if it hasn't already been shattered into a million pieces.

'Was it all a dream?' she'd asked Harry when she'd scooped him out of his cot this morning and his cheery smile had brought more tears to her eyes. Had the past weeks of blissfully happy marriage to Cortez been in her imagination? He'd made love to her with exquisite passion every night, but maybe for him it had only ever been sex, she thought bleakly. Without trust, passion was meaningless, a cruel parody of the marriage she yearned for.

She walked into the house and hurried upstairs to her old room to change out of her wet clothes. But, to her shock, she found the wardrobe empty. As she stared at the empty rails in disbelief, a gravelly voice came from behind her.

'I took the liberty of moving your things back to our bedroom.'

Elin spun round, and the sight of Cortez leaning nonchalantly against the doorframe released her from the terrible lethargy that had dulled her spirit and set her temper alight. It did not help that he looked as gorgeous as he always did in black jeans and a shirt, while the mirror over the dressing table revealed that she resembled a drowned rat.

'You have taken too many liberties,' she said in a hard voice, because pride was all she had left. 'I don't want to do this any more, Cortez.' It was the truth, she thought wearily. Loving him was destroying her.

He moved then, and as he came closer she was shocked by his grim expression. The gold flecks in his eyes were dulled and his skin was drawn tight over his slashing cheekbones so that he looked austere and beautiful, as if he'd spent the past twenty-four hours in hell, she realised with a jolt.

'Elin, I'm sorry,' he said roughly.

She closed her eyes to blot out his haggard face that made a fool of her because it gave her hope that he cared after all.

'I'm sorry too,' she whispered. 'For ever thinking that our crazy marriage could work.'

He flinched. 'It can work. It *did* work, until I screwed up.'

She shivered as the cold from her wet clothes seeped down to her bones, and heard him swear.

'You need a hot shower.'

'I'll have one when you've gone.' She gave a startled cry when he lifted her off her feet.

'Don't you get it? I'm not going anywhere, *querida*,' he told her fiercely as he carried her down the corridor to the master suite and strode straight into the bathroom. Elin tried to push his hands away when he set her on her feet and began to peel her sodden T-shirt over her head. But her body was trembling from the sweet pleasure of being in close proximity to him, and she did not have the strength of will to fight him when he tugged off her jeans and unfastened her bra. The hard peaks of her nipples betrayed her and she could not look at him, certain she would see mockery stamped on his hard features.

'How can you not know that I love you?' he said in an unsteady voice that *ached* with emotion.

Elin's eyes flew to his face and she felt her heart slam into her ribs when she saw the fierce intensity in his gaze. But she was afraid to believe.

'Don't make a joke of me,' she choked, hating the wretched tears that filled her eyes and clogged her throat. 'You drove away and left me.' She swallowed as he placed his thumb pads beneath her eyes and gently, oh, so gently wiped away the betraying moisture from her cheeks.

'Ah, Elin, *mi amor*,' he said huskily. 'How can you not know that I adore you, my innocent angel, *mi corazón,* when I told you every time I made love to you? With every kiss of my lips on yours and every caress with my hands and mouth I worshipped your body.'

She shook her head. 'That's just sex.' Her voice broke. 'You don't trust me.'

'I trust you with my life.' He turned on the shower taps, scooped her up and stood her beneath the spray, before he stripped off his clothes and joined her in the cubicle. Elin put her hand out to ward him off, but she had never been able to resist him, she thought with a flash of despair when he tugged her against him and held her so tight she could feel his heartbeat echo the pounding of hers.

'Tell me, my angel,' he said against her lips. 'Is this sex or love?' He kissed her mouth, her throat and paid homage to her breasts before he dropped to his knees and hooked her leg over his shoulder so that he could bestow the most intimate caress of all, while she sank against the shower wall and fell apart utterly with each stroke of his tongue.

He held her upright when her legs would have buckled with the intensity of her orgasm. And afterwards he soaped every inch of her body and washed her hair, gently kneading his fingers into her skull so that a simple hair-wash became erotic foreplay. He dried her with a soft towel and carried her through to the bedroom. When he laid her on the bed as if she was infinitely precious, Elin reached for him, needing him inside her as much as she needed to breathe oxygen.

But he lifted her hands from him and swiftly

kissed her to reassure her when he saw the betraying wobble of her mouth.

'My mother never got over her bitterness that my father had abandoned both of us before I was born,' he said sombrely. 'I grew up believing that trust was a fool's game. I was a hot-headed teenager and I frequently sought to defend my mother's honour with my fists. When another boy called my mother a whore, I went too far and one of my punches put him in hospital. I might have killed him, and rightly I would have spent the rest of my life in prison. Fortunately he recovered, but I'd learned that I must suppress my emotions and rely on my brain to secure a better life for my mother and myself.'

He stretched out beside her on the bed and drew her close so that her cheek was resting on his shoulder. 'My mother died the year I graduated from university and I moved to Madrid to work for Hernandez Bank. I was young, naïve—' he shrugged '—still grieving for the only person who had ever loved me. Whatever the reason, I fell hard for Alandra.'

Elin moved restively and he stroked her hair back from her face with a tenderness that made her tremble anew.

'When I discovered that Alandra had conceived my baby I wanted to marry her, but she told me she was engaged to a man who was richer than I was ever likely to be. I pleaded with her, and eventually she agreed to continue with the pregnancy and to be my wife.' His face darkened. 'I believed her when she said she was going home to break the news to her parents. Three days later she called me from Toronto. Her visa had come through, and she informed me that she had got rid of the baby before flying out to join her fiancé.'

'Oh, Cortez,' Elin said softly. 'No wonder you were so angry when you caught me trying to drive away from La Casa Jazmín with Harry. I swear I had decided not to leave because I knew you loved him and I couldn't take him away from you.'

'I was angrier with myself. I'd done everything wrong with you. It's no defence but, a month before I met you, Alandra turned up at my office. I hadn't seen her for ten years. She told me that the guy she'd married hadn't made as much money as she'd hoped, while I had become a millionaire. She had left her husband and she suggested we could get back together. She would even have my child if I was still "hooked on fatherhood"—her words, not mine,' he said grimly. 'Needless to say, I turned down her offer, but the episode made me wonder why I'd been so stupid to fall in love with her, and I was determined never to allow another woman to have power over me.'

He slid a finger beneath Elin's chin and tipped her face towards his. 'After Alandra, I vowed that I would never give my trust so easily again. But I took one look at you and I was lost. I didn't want to fall in love with you,' he said rawly. 'It was convenient to believe the stories in the tabloids and convince myself that you could not have been as innocent as my heart insisted you were.'

Cortez lifted himself on top of her and trapped her gaze with his, and the wealth of emotion, of *love* reflected in his eyes caused Elin to catch her breath. 'When I found out that Harry was mine, I was overwhelmed with guilt that I had abandoned you, like Ralph Saunderson abandoned my mother. I didn't know how you could forgive me, let alone love me,' he said roughly.

In that instant everything that had seemed so complicated and hopeless became blindingly simple. So simple that Elin wondered how it had taken them so long to realise what had happened on her birthday night over a year ago. Some people said that love at first sight couldn't happen, but she knew for certain it could. It had. For both of them.

'There is nothing to forgive,' she said softly. 'You are a wonderful father to Harry and everything you have done has been for him.'

'That's not quite true, *querida*. I coerced and threatened you into marrying me because you are the only woman I will ever love.' Cortez swallowed convulsively and Elin blinked back her tears when she saw the betraying glitter in his eyes. 'Do you love me?' he muttered, revealing a vulnerability that made her love him all the more.

'With all my heart. I will love you for ever.' Taking him by surprise, she pushed him onto his back and straddled him, loving the way his eyes gleamed with golden flames when he guided her down onto his erection. 'Is this love or sex?' she whispered against his mouth.

'Ask me again after a lifetime,' he murmured. 'I want to share love and laughter, friendship and trust with you for the rest of our lives, my angel.'

And Elin thought the future sounded blissful.

* * * * *

If you enjoyed reading Elin's passionate love story
THE SAUNDERSON LEGACY *continues with*

THE THRONE HE MUST TAKE
Coming September 2017!

In the meantime why not explore these other
Chantelle Shaw stories?

MISTRESS OF HIS REVENGE
MASTER OF HER INNOCENCE
TRAPPED BY VIALLI'S VOWS
ACQUIRED BY HER GREEK BOSS
Available now!

Get 2 Free Books,
<u>Plus</u> 2 Free Gifts—
just for trying the Reader Service!

SPECIAL EXCERPT FROM

❋ HARLEQUIN
™

Presents®

*Natasha Pellegrini and Matteo Manaserro's reunion
catches them both in a potent mix of emotion, and they
surrender to their explosive passion. Natasha was a
virgin until Matteo's touch branded her as his and
when Matteo discovers Natasha is pregnant,
he's intent on claiming his baby. Except he hasn't
bargained on their insatiable chemistry binding them
together so completely!*

Read on for a sneak preview of
Michelle Smart's *book*
CLAIMING HIS ONE-NIGHT BABY,
the second part of her
BOUND TO A BILLIONAIRE *trilogy.*

"Come to Miami with me. I'm flying to Caballeros with
Daniele tomorrow. We should be there for only a couple of
days. When I get back I'll take you home with me. We can
say you need a break from everything. In a month or so we
can tell them you're pregnant with my child. It'll be easier
for them to accept we turned to each other for comfort and
that a relationship grew naturally than to accept the truth of
the child's conception."

"You want us to lie?"

"No, I do not want us to lie. I despise dishonesty but
what's the alternative? Do you want to return to your parents
in England and…"

"No." Her rebuttal was emphatic.

"Then coming with me is the only answer. If you stay in Pisa, and Vanessa and the others think there is even a chance you are carrying Pieta's… To build their hopes up only to cut them away would be too cruel. We need to show a united front starting from now."

"So you do accept the baby's yours?"

"Yes. I accept it's mine and I will acknowledge it as mine. Come with me and I will protect you both, and we will have a small chance of making the pain of what's to come a little less in the family who has shown both of us nothing but love and acceptance. They have suffered enough."

She rested her head against the window and closed her eyes. He hated that even looking as if she hadn't slept in a month she was still the most beautiful woman he'd ever laid eyes on.

Eventually she nodded. "Okay," she said in her soft, clear voice. "I'll come to Miami with you. But only for a while. We can fake a burgeoning relationship, I can get pregnant and then we can split up."

"We stay together until it's born."

Her eyes flew open to stare at him with incredulity. "That's seven and a half months away."